SHOOTERS

SHOOTERS

TERRILL LANKFORD

A TOM DOHERTY ASSOCIATES BOOK

NEW YORK

SHOOTERS

A Forge Book
Published by Tom Doherty Associates, Inc.
175 Fifth Avenue
New York, NY 10010

Forge® is a registered trademark of Tom Doherty Associates, Inc.

Design by Ann Gold

Library of Congress Cataloging-in-Publication Data

Lankford, Terrill.
Shooters /   Terrill Lankford.
p.   cm.
"A Tom Doherty Associates book."
ISBN 0-312-86272-5
I.   Title.
PS3562.A542S48   1997
813'.54—dc20   96-29344
                                                      CIP

First Edition: February 1997

Printed in the United States of America

0 9 8 7 6 5 4 3 2 1

To Arch and Babs.

You were right.
Experience is the major textbook.

ACKNOWLEDGMENTS

Special thanks must go to Carol McCleary, Bob Gleason, Tom Doherty and Ben Cosgrove, the Four Horsepeople of the Apocalypse, without whom this book would not exist, to Steve de las Heras, for performing heroic acts far above and beyond the call of duty, and to Stephen Collins, Jolina Mitchell-Collins and Paul Buckley, who provided the initial spark and inspiration that got this ball rolling over a decade ago.

The past is always with you.
　　　　　　　　—Nick Gardner

SHOOTERS

PROLOGUE

They say history is written by the victors, the winners. Not this time. This bit of history will be chronicled by one of the great losers of all time, namely—me. But trust that you will receive the unfiltered truth, as only a true loser could deliver. Untarnished by the need to appear heroic in any way, shape, or form. I want to explain it all to you. Every last grimy detail. Every evil notion, every weak moment. I feel I owe it to you. And if not to you, then to myself and to the people who got hurt when all this went down. I want to spare no one in my text, not even myself, so my language may be graphic, crude at times, but when I am finished I hope you will have a better understanding of the circumstances that led up to my current sorry state of affairs. The ridiculousness of it all, really. The story I'm about to tell you may seem outlandish in detail, but I assure you it is all true. I plan on leaving nothing out. No brutal action will be left unaccounted for, no wicked thought that can be remembered will be censored. This could be considered pandering at its worst, but you must bear with this crude exercise if you are to understand the truth about what happened in the fall of last year.

This story is a by-product of the eighties, the Reagan years, when the wrong people made a lot of money the wrong way. I was one of those people. The seventies had been rough. The late-seventies recession made work in my chosen profession—photography—difficult. When the economy opened up a few years later, I didn't stop to ask stupid questions, I started panning up the ore like every other jerk. I never thought about the mine playing out or someone showing up with a huge bill. I felt charmed. I thought I was some kind of fucking genius.

I was a smart-ass know-it-all living the American dream. From rags to riches, from Volkswagen to Lamborghini, from one-room dive in New York City to sprawling beach house in Malibu, California. I had become a living cliché, the guy you hate as he passes you at ninety on the freeway, but secretly you envy him and his foreign car and the blond sex machine in the passenger seat. Secretly you wish you could be that guy. You wish you could live his life. But you can't. That's *his* life. The thing I hadn't bargained on as I cruised through the fat eighties into the strange nineties was the simple fact that the past has a memory. The past never goes away. The past does not forget. And the past does not forgive.

The past is always with you.

PART I

You think you've got it all figured out, don't you, Nick?
—Jennifer Joyner

1

In the cool darkness of the garage I found a random tape and slapped it into the cassette player. The Doors' "L.A. Woman" drifted out of the speakers as the garage door opened, revealing the Pacific Coast Highway in Malibu. *PCH* as it's known to the nine million denizens of Los Angeles county. I revved the engine of my car, a black Lamborghini Diablo I had picked up used a few months earlier, trying to warm it to the point that I would feel safe attempting intercourse with noonday traffic. I lived near the south end of a tightly knit strip of six- and seven-figure homes wedged between PCH and the Pacific Ocean. There was barely six feet separating the adjoining houses from each other and PCH was almost as close to our back doors as our neighboring houses were to either side of us. My driveway was a short eight-foot pour of asphalt that connected the garage directly to PCH. Merging with the speeding traffic was usually a tricky maneuver. I waited for my moment, then pulled out into the lane fast and quickly accelerated with the driving beat of "L.A. Woman" blasting our ears.

My name is Nick Gardner, although names at this stage of

the game are not as important as you might think. I'm thirty-five years young and have the liver of a fifty-year-old wino. Some people consider me attractive, but these are not necessarily people with good taste. Most think I'm cold. It's something I work hard at. Even if you could have seen behind my jet-black shades you wouldn't have found a trace of emotion in my eyes. On this hot October day my hair was slicked back tight for minimum wind resistance. That's my preferred style. Neat, orderly, immovable. And today was like any other day. I was cool, calm, and detached. Everything was under perfect control. My world was in order.

Jennifer Joyner, however, was a different story. She was sitting in the passenger seat of the Lamborghini. The top was off the car and the wind was trying to tear the scarf away from her three-hundred-dollar perm. Control was not in Jennifer's vocabulary. She was a thrill junkie. One hundred five pounds of raw nerve endings. She loved going fast. She ate road speed like others eat ice cream. Not much could impress her short of spinning out at the Indy 500.

As we sped along PCH we could see smoke hanging over the city far in the distance. The hot Santa Ana winds had hit town and drained all the humidity out of the air. Los Angeles had experienced a massive amount of rainfall a few months earlier, after more than five years of extreme drought. Vegetation had suddenly run amuck, and now that vegetation was very dry. These conditions had combined to create a powder keg. An arsonist's sense of humor was all the fuse that was needed. Some asshole had set half of Thousand Oaks on fire with a butane lighter just to see it burn. The spectacular news coverage of houses and trees burning out of control had inspired three other arsonists to join in the fun. Two in Thousand Oaks and one all the way down in Laguna Beach. The fires had already been burning for two days and no end was in sight. Leave it up to the news guys to bring gasoline to a forest fire.

I took a left onto Sunset Boulevard. The road twisted and turned at seventy miles an hour in front of our eyes. I had trimmed ten off the speedometer in deference to the winding nature of Sunset, but it wasn't enough. A slow-moving Audi appeared abruptly in front of us. I downshifted, then in a sudden burst of speed passed the Audi and jumped back into the proper lane a split second before an oncoming black Caddy roared past us, blaring its horn. I saw you, buddy. I saw you.

Jennifer was loving the speed, head back, laughing, thrilling as I weaved in and out of traffic on the twisting snake of a road. There was no fear in her. She had absolute confidence that we could not die.

Sure, I've slept with other photographers, but I never got involved with them. Nick does something for me that those other guys don't. He's exciting. It's more like being with a rock star than a photographer. He's got such an aloofness. It's a turn-on, but it can be kind of maddening too. For some guys the distant bit is just an act. But not Nick. When he tells you to get out of his hair, he means it.

—Jennifer Joyner

Jennifer reached over and grabbed my crotch, massaging it appreciatively. Finding it responsive, she shifted gears herself. She unzipped my fly and pulled my cock free. She stroked it a few times, then just couldn't help sampling it in her mouth.

The car being open, more than a few fellow travelers noticed Jennifer's head bob up and down as we ripped past them. The ultimate in wealthy arrogance. A slicked-out asshole getting head in his Lamborghini as he weaved in and out of traffic at almost twice the legal speed limit.

I have to admit the sad spectacle of it all gave me some sense of perverse pleasure. We were a sick joke hurtling through space at seventy mph. Unfortunately, great art requires a great audience. I did not notice many people laughing in the cars we were passing.

We were rapidly approaching the Sunset/Sepulveda intersection. The traffic light was red for Sunset, but I didn't slow down. I actually went faster. As Jennifer licked and sucked my cock I just couldn't find it in my heart to apply the brakes. Cars were traveling through the light on Sepulveda in an intermittent pattern. It looked like there was going to be a collision!

I came just as we hit the intersection. Jennifer sat up, saw what was happening, screamed, and squeezed my spurting cock hard with both hands, splattering my Hugo Boss suit. I shot through the space between two cars and slammed on the brakes, skidding to a stop on the side of the road. Cars screeched and tires smoked as everyone attempted to avoid a chain reaction. People skidded to a halt, narrowly avoiding the bumper of the vehicle in front of them.

I was shaken. I didn't know what had come over me. Did I want to kill us? Did I want to kill others? Or was I just trying to get a reaction out of Jennifer? A hint of some true emotion other than animal passion? I don't know if I did it on purpose or just blanked out. The whole scene felt like a dream. Someone else's dream that I had somehow entered. Maybe it wasn't Jennifer's humanity I was testing. Maybe it was mine.

2

We were an hour late to the studio. I was supposed to be shooting stills, we call them chromes, for a perfume ad. The perfume, ironically enough, was called Collision, and there were two full-size sports cars on the set, bumper to bumper, in front of a backdrop of a desolate city scape. A building in the center of the backdrop was shaped like a giant perfume bottle with the name *Collision* written across the front in office lights.

Salvatore, my art director, had done another brilliant job. Of course when the ad saw print everyone would assume *I* was the genius. Hey, I *hired* him.

I had an espresso while Jennifer got dressed and had her makeup done. Everyone else was there, waiting on us. I gave no apology. They were being paid well whether they worked or not. Lou Collins, my partner, walked by and pointed at his watch with a wry smile. I smiled back and shrugged. Partner up with a horny photographer, be ready to pay some OT.

After an hour or so, Jennifer came out of the dressing room.

"I'm ready, stud," she said jokingly, but also loudly enough for everybody in a three-mile radius to hear her.

She knew how much something like that would perturb me and it worked. I was pissed off before the first shot clicked over. She was going to fuck with me to make up for almost killing her on the drive over. She also wanted to lay a not-so-subtle claim so that the other models we had in for the day wouldn't try to jostle her out of pole position.

I always tried not to get involved with the models, but I'm weak and they're beautiful and usually calloused enough to deal with the apathy that comes with seeing me on anything other than professional terms. Some of them just want what I want—a good clean fuck. No hassles. No involvements. No intrigues. Jennifer started out like that, but lately she was showing signs of moral disintegration. She was beginning to get possessive, to act like we were developing into "a couple." This called for a readjustment. She was setting herself up for "the talk." And that would be the end of that.

Too bad. I enjoyed the sex. Occasionally even enjoyed her company, which surprised me. Models usually had little of interest to say. They were too concerned with diets and hairstyles and who's fucking who and how you blow your way onto the cover of *Cosmo*.

But Jennifer was a little different. She watched the six o'clock news faithfully, rooted for the Phoenix Suns after they picked up Charles Barkley, and even read a book on occasion.

She knew exactly who she was.

Her ambitions were limited to modeling. None of that acting shit that so many of the girls tried to segue into. She was happy to pose without words, collect the checks, and pay for her condo on the west side. When she got older she planned on starting her own modeling agency.

I had been sleeping with Jennifer for about five months, on and off, ever since the first day we worked together. We did a suntan oil piece down on Venice Beach and I knew from the moment we locked eyes that we were going to tangle. She was just my type, long and leggy with curly dark hair down

past her shoulders. She had sparkling green eyes, high cheek-
bones—standard on this model—and full lips that didn't need
any collagen injections to give them depth. Her bottom lip
gave her the look of a continuous pout unless she was smiling, which was most of the time; then she looked like a walking, talking magazine cover. I could take her once or twice a
week, four or five hours at a time, but we'd been seeing each
other a little too much lately. Fault lines were beginning to
show in the structure.

    We had met at the Rose Cafe the night before the Colli-
sion shoot, ostensibly to discuss the layout, but Jennifer
Joyner doesn't take no for an answer once she begins a se-
duction, and the night led to an early morning full of carnal
bliss capped off with the blow job that almost killed us on
Sunset Boulevard. I was already exhausted and a bit full of
Jennifer by the time we began shooting, but she was doing
everything in her power to keep me riled up and interested
in her. She knew her limitations and could sense mine.

    Within a half hour we had the setup ready to be pho-
tographed. A man in a three-piece suit and a woman in a
slinky evening gown argued seductively in front of the automobiles. Jennifer was dressed in a supershort and skimpy
black leather cop uniform complete with storm trooper boots
and hooker garters. She mimed writing a "love ticket" while
standing above the two models with one foot on the trunk of
the front car and one foot on the hood of the rear car. I had
Whitney, my main camera assistant, slap some early eighties
Bauhaus on the sound system to get the juices flowing. The
place was rocking with black death and hot sex. The mood was
just right.

    I worked the set, shooting from a very deliberate series of
angles and giving brief one- and two-word suggestions to the

models. They performed like the living mannequins they
were and gave me just what I wanted. Total ego, total greedy
sexuality. But it wasn't enough. It felt wrong. It was all rote.
Bloodless.

By the time the session was over, I was beat. I couldn't
focus anymore and I had lost all notion of what the campaign
was about. We had done everything required by the ad agency
that had commissioned the job, but something was missing.
Some spark. No one on this set was horny yet and if you can't
get a hard-on when you're doing the setup, the buyer ain't
gonna get one when he looks at the ad, and that means you're
not going to move your product to the consumer.

I decided to think about it overnight and ordered everyone back in the morning, much to Lou's consternation. He
thought we could get it all in one day. We were being paid a
flat rate. Whatever we spent on the shoot came out of our
end. Being the greedy little businessman he was, he didn't
want to spend the extra money.

Lou made a few sad noises about it all, but he knew better than to push it. The artist rules at this stage of the game.
He was hell on wheels when it came to negotiating the deals,
but when it came to the space between me, the camera, and
my subjects, he didn't fuck around. That was our deal from
the beginning of our three-year partnership and he had remained faithful to that aspect of our relationship, no matter
how much it cost the company. We always came out ahead in
the long run. Just not as far ahead as Lou wanted.

As I was wrapping my equipment I could see the two "driver" models talking in the background, setting up a dinner
date. A few camera assistants and stagehands were milling
around, doing various jobs at a leisurely pace. It had been an

easy day for them. The kind of day that usually doesn't produce the desired results. It hadn't.

Jennifer approached me. She was now dressed in tights. She wiped sweat off her neck with a black towel and purred, "What's on for tonight, Nick?" in a way that told me she had something very specific in mind.

"No plans," I responded before I had a chance to think about it. I did not usually make a habit of seeing the same woman two nights in a row. It was a bad policy that could lead to trouble.

"There's a Halloween party at Mark Pecchia's," Jennifer said.

"Who's Mark Pecchia?"

"You know, the rock video director."

"Never heard of him." I *had* heard of Pecchia, but I wasn't about to let her know it. I didn't want to go to any party at some hipper-than-thou video director's sleaze pit.

"C'mon, it'll be fun," she chimed.

"I'm not much of a partier."

"Unless it's *your* party."

"Right."

"I want to go." She played with my tie, trying to minx it up a bit.

The manipulation was in full swing and I wasn't going to put up with it. It was time to start lowering the boom. I looked at her with my blankest stare and said, "Who's stopping you?"

Jennifer's face dropped.

"You are such a cold fuck."

I turned and walked away from her. I began removing a lens from one of my cameras and realized she was right behind me. The stoic shoulder hadn't worked.

"You think you've got it all figured out, don't you, Nick? I'm not just another one of your disposable models. I'm a *real* person! You can't just use me when you want me, then throw me on the trash heap!"

This was starting to draw attention. It was the kind of publicity that I didn't welcome. I took a step closer to Jennifer so no one else would hear what I had to say. I had to come up with something to cool her off before she really went ballistic. Jennifer had a temper, but that's what made her special in front of the camera and in bed as well. This "special" quality had a tendency to backfire at times. I decided to exercise a rare bit of diplomacy.

"I'm sorry," I said. "I didn't mean it the way it sounded. I'm just stressed out over this job. I don't think I've got a hold on it yet and it's pissing me off."

It was as close to the truth as I could come without increasing her anger. I *was* pissed off at the job, but she was pissing me off even more.

Jennifer was suddenly concerned about her performance. All thought of personal feelings was gone, tucked away behind the brick wall of career. She was a seasoned pro, through and through.

"You think it's *us?*" She meant the other models, of course, not her, but she was showing a rare bit of diplomacy herself.

"No, no, no. . . . You guys are doing great. It's me. This campaign needs something more. Something special. Something I'm not seeing."

"You should come to the party, then. The crowd'll be wild. Could be good inspiration."

"I get all the inspiration I need driving home at night."

"C'mon, Nick. Don't be such a recluse."

"I really can't, Jenn. I'm wasted. Burnt to a crisp."

I turned away and continued wrapping out my equipment.

Jennifer pouted more sullenly than usual, like a six-year-old trying to get her way. I looked at her and thought about it for a moment. She was pretty funny at times. I involuntarily snorted a little laugh.

"You know how I like to see you pout."

"I'm not asking you to marry me or anything. I just thought you might like to go to a party. As friends. No strings attached."

I did something stupid and unusual. I gave in.

"What time do you want me to pick you up?"

Jennifer brightened. "Eightish."

She kissed me on the cheek and said, "Thanks".

I felt awkward. I was not accustomed to displays of emotion, no matter how simple. I'd much rather have sex with a complete stranger than kiss a friend with meaning. I mumbled, "Uh-huh," and went back to packing up as Jennifer scurried off to change.

3

I fought the rush-hour traffic and got back home by six-thirty. My house on PCH was high-tech, yet minimally furnished. I was never much for collecting possessions. I think it gives one a false sense of permanence. I've always lived spartanly, almost Japanese in style and simplicity. I had no more than was needed to make things comfortable, but what I did have was the very best. The best couches and chairs from Italy, the best bedroom furnishings from Denmark, the best dining room layout from Japan, and the best kitchenware from France. My decorator had taken the simplest styles from each of these countries and designed an interior that had symmetry and class. It sounds like it would be schizophrenic, a tour through the United Nations, but it wasn't. She found just the right pieces to complement the whole and make it all work, as if a new race of people had been discovered using the finest these countries had to offer and discarding the rest.

The setting sun cast an amber glow throughout my house as I entered and dropped my satchel by the door. The beach side of the house was all glass, floor-to-ceiling windows throughout. The PCH side was thick concrete block and various soundproofing materials to muffle the traffic noise. It worked wonders. The sound of waves cascading on the beach easily drowned out the stream of traffic flowing eight feet outside the front door.

I collapsed into a chair and stared through the blinds at the ocean. An orange fireball reflected off the Malibu surf. Another day was shot. I'd never get it back. And how had I spent my lost day? The same way I spent the last three thousand days. Taking pictures. Burning film for some advertising house trying to sell the public twenty cents of stink for thirty dollars an ounce. Somewhere on the planet people were doing something worthwhile. I did not know these people.

I watched the ocean devour the sun and wondered what the night would bring. I was so fed up with "the scene." L.A. was growing stuffy for me. I was feeling the itch. I had a touch of wanderlust. Or maybe it was nerves. Things had been going smoothly for too long. I could feel something coming, waiting around the corner to pounce. For months I had had the uneasy feeling of a gambler who had stayed at the same blackjack table for too long. The smart operators know when it's time to make a move. I had my eye on the door, I just couldn't seem to be able to get out of my own way.

PART II

Risk increases exponentially with beauty.

—Nick Gardner

1

I picked Jennifer Joyner up at a little after eight. We drove slowly into Beverly Hills. I was in no hurry to get to this party. Jennifer's eyes were red and I could tell that she'd been crying. I asked her what was wrong.

"I took a nap when I got home," she said flatly. "I had a dream and when I woke up I was crying."

"What was the dream about?"

"It was nonsense. You don't want to hear it. It's boring."

"We've got time."

"You won't believe it."

"Shock me."

"In the dream I'm living with someone in a tiny house out in the country. It's beautiful. The house is like a dollhouse, white picket fence and everything. The countryside is spectacular and there are no houses anywhere except for ours."

"Ours?"

"Mine and the guy I live with in the dream. Don't worry, Nick, it's not you. It's not anyone. I can never see his face clearly, but he's got a gorgeous body. He's the perfect man.

Great body, no face, no mouth. And he loves me. We're happy. Incredibly happy, living out in the country in our little dollhouse, ready to raise kids, protected by our little white picket fence. Corny, huh?"

"What happened?" I asked. "Why did you cry?"

"I woke up."

2

Mark Pecchia lived in Benedict Canyon, up where old money habitated side by side with the nouveaux riches. It was an impressive neighborhood. You had to be some breed of shark to buy into that pond. I pulled up in front of a very large house that used to belong to Errol Flynn. A long line of expensive vehicles were parked along the side of the street, stretching far up the hill in front of us.

A young white guy in a Jack Pick's Parking uniform opened the door for me. I recognized the kid from a half dozen parties I'd been at in the last year. His name tag read Daniel, but I knew him as Clyde Vogel. He had changed his name recently at the suggestion of his talent agent.

"Take it easy on her, Clyde," I warned.

"I treat this car like it's my own," Clyde sang, like he was auditioning for an opera.

"That's what I'm afraid of."

A similarly dressed Latino attendant opened Jennifer's door and helped her out, copping a little feel as he made his move. She lived with it.

Clyde gave me a ticket stub, got into the Lamborghini and burned rubber up the hill.

I looked at the other attendant and handed him a ten. I had seen this guy parking cars at parties for the last three years, but I still didn't know his name. He never wore a name tag and never offered to reveal his identity. He was friendly enough, but he seemed to want to remain anonymous. Probably another failed actor thinking he should protect his name for the big time. Not spread it around so everybody remembers him as what's-his-name, the parking attendant. I respect a person's privacy, so I never pushed him on his identity. He folded the ten and smiled at me appreciatively.

"Tell your buddy not to race anything faster than a Porsche in my car tonight," I said. "It needs a tune-up."

"Will do."

Jennifer and I walked toward the house. A big, beefy fucker was standing at the door to make sure only the elite entered. He gave Jennifer a kiss on the neck, which I took as a good sign, then he ushered us in without a word.

The place was a sparse, half-decorated minimansion packed with every type of Hollywood scum in the catalog. Many of them were dressed in outlandish Halloween costumes, many had just come as they were in real life. It was a minimal difference.

Either Mark Pecchia and I had similar tastes in decorating or he had bought into something he couldn't quite pay for. The town is full of people who buy or rent big houses for show, then don't have enough money left to buy a chair to squat on. There are people driving sixty-thousand-dollar automobiles who can't pay the rent on their five-hundred-dollar-a-month apartments. It's all a show. It's flash and front. Runners going long, hoping for the miracle pass and a winning touchdown. In these neighborhoods you didn't have to keep up with the Joneses if you were going to stay in business, you had to keep up with the Rockefellers and Bill Cosby.

Pecchia had about half the furniture one would expect in

a place this size. I couldn't tell if it was on purpose or out of poverty. The stuff he had was nice, what could be seen of it. The place was filled with wall-to-wall bodies. What decor could be seen appeared to be Santa Fe stuff trying to blend with the classic Spanish design of the house. Pecchia probably picked the furniture up cheap at a Beverly Hills yard sale in the late eighties as the style slipped out of vogue.

The lighting was low in the auditorium-sized living room, the average moral attitude even lower. They had rounded up the usual suspects, plus half of Santa Monica Boulevard. The room was a steaming sea of tattoos and pierced flesh, black leather and torn lace. Jennifer and I moved through the crowd and mingled. It was frightening how easily we blended in.

Jennifer pulled me toward a tall man with long hair, beard, mustache, blue jeans, pink shirt, red tie, and hipster sunglasses. He had an imported beer in one hand, a joint in the other. It had to be the host.

"Mark!" Jennifer exclaimed as she kissed him on the cheek.

"Hey, JJ," the man responded with utter cool. JJ was not something I had ever heard anyone call Jennifer Joyner. I hoped I wouldn't hear it again.

"Mark, I want you to meet a friend of mine . . . Nick Gardner."

Pecchia put the joint in his mouth and shook my hand vigorously.

"Glad you could make it, Nick. I really like your stuff."

I was a little taken aback by that statement, but I mumbled "Thanks," and nodded like an idiot.

Pecchia offered me the joint. "Hit?"

"No thanks."

Pecchia grabbed the arm of an overweight guy who was

breezing past and stopped him in his tracks.

"Morrie, get Nick and Jennifer something from the bar," Pecchia commanded.

"Sure thing," the chunky guy bubbled. He seemed accustomed to kissing ass. He appeared to *enjoy* it.

"What are you drinking, Nick?" Pecchia asked.

"Jack Daniel's straight up will be fine."

"JJ?"

"I'll just have a diet Coke."

"Be right back," Morrie said, skipping off like an obedient bunny.

Mark turned me around and walked me through the crowd. Jennifer trailed along, her eyes scanning the room for potential pleasures and thrills.

"I gotta be real honest, Nick," Mark said. "I've ripped you off, man."

"What?"

"Your images, guy. I've been so blown away by your images that I've used some of your stuff in my videos. I hope you haven't been too pissed off."

It took me a second to even understand what he was saying. Why should I give a fuck if he stole some print idea of mine for his stupid videos? This guy was vain. I decided to give a little attitude back in return.

"I have to be honest with you, too, Mark. I haven't *seen* your videos. I don't watch videos."

"You don't watch videos? How do you come up with your ideas? I mean, like, we're all interconnected, right? I mean, we all basically do the same things, you know? Blow people's minds into buying our products."

"I suppose," I said. The guy was creeping me out. He was some weird hybrid of a character. He seemed to be all the worst elements of the sixties, seventies, and eighties rolled up in one pretentious package for the nineties.

"You bet," he continued relentlessly. "When I first saw your stuff I said, 'Now here's a guy that ought to be directing fucking videos!' I mean, your shit just blew me away. That stocking ad you did last year, the overhead shot with the chicks and the razor blades . . ."

"Shear Wear?"

"Yeah, that's the one. . . . Well, I was on a Megakill video and we were all ready to shoot and first thing on the set that day I open a magazine and see that ad. . . . I just said, 'Fuck it,' canceled the shoot, and reworked the concept using that kind of imagery. I won a fucking MTV award on that video. You're the best there is, Nick. You're my inspiration."

Jennifer seemed proud that I was getting all this praise from Pecchia. I felt embarrassed. I don't like compliments and I particularly don't like compliments from people like Mark Pecchia.

Morrie appeared with the drinks and distributed them properly.

"Thanks," I said.

Morrie nodded at me, then stood waiting for Pecchia to tell him what to do next.

"Disappear" was the command.

Morrie moved off like a good slave. I felt very uncomfortable about the whole exchange. Jennifer noticed and I think she understood. I don't give a lot of emotion to the people I work with, but I try not to shit on them either. There was a different set of ethics at play around here.

Pecchia moved us through the party like Gandhi among the true believers.

"You've got quite a crowd here," I said.

Pecchia laughed. "They're animals. . . . It'll get worse before it gets better."

Pecchia glad-handed a few of his minions, and a buxom blonde in a tight-fitting Catwoman outfit suddenly grabbed me by the arm and turned me around.

"Nicky!" she squealed. "What the fuck are you doing here?"

I experienced a moment of confusion. I wasn't even sure where I knew this girl from, although I knew I *had* slept with her. She was a model, of course, and a pretty hot number as models go. I just couldn't put a name on the body. Whoever she was, I didn't want to get in the middle of a *real* catfight between her and Jennifer. I stumbled around for an answer to her question, which, by the way, was a good one. What the fuck *was* I doing here?

"I . . . uh . . . Jennifer invited me," I stammered.

She didn't miss a beat or give a shit who I was with. "That's great," she said. "Listen, you've got to meet my girlfriend, Sarah. I told her all about you."

"I . . . um . . ."

I looked at Jennifer, who smiled knowingly and nodded her approval. The girl looked at Jennifer with appreciation.

"Thanks. I'll only steal him for a minute."

"Do what you have to do," Jennifer said with a faux smile.

The girl started to drag me away into the crowd. She was still gabbing. "Shit, Nicky, what happened to you? You haven't called me in months. . . ."

I could see Pecchia and Jennifer talking as I was towed through the mob. Pecchia leaned in close to Jennifer and whispered something into her ear. She didn't laugh, so I assumed he wasn't trying to pick her up. Actually they looked quite serious, considering this was a party. Los Angeles. Business is a twenty-four-hour-a-day process here.

3

Twenty minutes later I was sitting off in a corner, nursing a drink, watching the crowd. The party had long since zipped past the point of novelty for me. I had been to a lot of parties like this but not lately. It was a pre-AIDS atmosphere. Lots of drugs. Lots of loose sex being negotiated. Halloween usually brought this kind of behavior out of a crowd, but this bunch didn't need any prodding.

Jennifer was laughing it up in the middle of the room with a bunch of black-clad rock and rollers. She looked funny, all slinked out in a sheer white evening gown amid these Hell's Angels rejects.

My attention was drawn to the bar. Mark Pecchia stood there talking to the most voluptuous woman in the room, possibly any room. Long blond hair, full round breasts, more curves than Mulholland Drive. She wore a simple shirtdress, no jewelry, just a belt cinching it all tight, torturing the male population. She made the other women in the room look like men and made the men in the room feel like little boys.

I got to my feet and walked through the crowd toward the bar. Pecchia saw me coming and grinned like a reptile baking on a rock. He had something great for show and tell.

"Nick, buddy, where you been hiding?" he asked. "I was lookin' for you."

"Here I am."

The girl and I got into an eye lock. There were immediate sparks.

"Nick, have you met Candice?" Pecchia asked.

"No," I muttered.

Candice extended her hand. I took it and held it, not really shaking it, just holding it, feeling her presence from my head to my toes. I felt like I was already inside of her and I could tell by her expression that she was reading my mind.

"Nick Gardner, Candice Bishop, Candy this is Nick." Pecchia was talking, but I was no longer paying attention to him. I was totally focused on the woman.

"Pleased to meet you, Nick. Mark was just telling me about your work. It sounds very exciting. . . ." Her voice was soft and fragile, like crystal on the verge of breaking.

Pecchia took my empty glass from me. "You're dry, babe," he said. "We can't have any of that around here. What was it again?"

"Jack Daniel's straight up," I said robotically, still mesmerized by Candice Bishop.

Pecchia turned to the bartender, receiving immediate service.

"Jack straight."

The bartender nodded, took the glass, and began pouring.

———

You got to understand, this guy Nick was a real hero of mine. He did shit with his photography that would have given Nagel a hard-on. I "borrowed" from him—sometimes without even knowing it. He did some chromes of black chicks for a Nike ad, for chrissakes, and I jacked off to 'em. Can you believe that? Jacking off on a Nike ad?

—Mark Pecchia

———

Pecchia turned to me and said, "Candice has done some modeling, Nick. Think you could use her sometime?"

"Definitely."

"I haven't done fashion in years and when I did it was in Europe," Candice said. "I've been told I don't have the right look for print in the States. They say I'm too big."

I knew what she meant. She was no string bean. She was like a healthy Swedish girl, big boned and voluptuous. A *Playboy* layout maybe, a harder sell to the anorectic set looking to buy jeans.

"You need the right project," I said.

The bartender slid my drink in front of me. It was tall, wide, and deep.

Pecchia looked off into the crowd and saw someone with whom he wanted to connect. He seemed to have no proprietary attitude toward Candice.

"You two get acquainted," he said. "I've got to say hello to some people." Pecchia moved off. Candice and I sipped our drinks and looked each other over.

"What are you thinking?" Candice asked.

"I was just wondering how long I could be under your shirt before I was dragged away and beaten by the mob."

"If you're careful, maybe no one would notice."

Our eyes locked again. I felt electrical fire between us. There was going to be trouble. I wanted to take her right then and there. Just bend her over the bar and start slamming.

"Are you here with anyone?" I asked.

"A friend. And you?"

"A friend."

"Would your friend be able to get home if we left without her?"

"She'd probably end up going home with *your* friend," I said.

"Do you have any coke?"

"No." I didn't like drugs. Didn't do them and never carried them, even knowing that they were quite often the currency with which attractive young women preferred to trade.

"Can you get some?" she asked. "Can you get us some coke?"

I looked at Candice for a moment and calculated the risks involved with this encounter and weighed them against the possible returns. She was dangerous. More trouble than it could possibly be worth. Then again, it looked like it could be worth quite a bit. What the hell. I searched the crowd, looking for Mark Pecchia. If someone around here was going to hook me up, it would be him. I spotted him leaving the room.

"Confidence is high," I said to Candice.

I walked through the living room and down a crowded hallway in pursuit of Mark Pecchia. The hall was a gauntlet of men and women of all varieties and combinations smoking, drinking, talking, making out. I stopped in front of a closed bathroom door and leaned against the opposite wall. I could hear Pecchia talking in the bathroom. Peals of female laughter punctuated his commentary. I lit up a cigarette and waited.

I slowly became aware of moaning coming from the bedroom behind me. I looked at the door. It was open a crack. I eased the door open a little more. The lights were on in the bedroom. A long-haired musician type in a werewolf outfit was giving it to a young girl on top of a coat-covered bed. If the girl was eighteen, it wasn't by much. She *had* been dressed as Little Red Riding Hood, but most of her costume had been torn away by the big bad werewolf in his attempt to consume her. I guess she was getting what she asked for.

I stared in at the activity. It was nothing I hadn't done or seen before, sans costumes of course. I was transfixed, nevertheless.

The bathroom door suddenly opened. Mark Pecchia stepped out, dusting his mustache and beard. I could see two young girls in the bathroom, still going at some coke remnants on a mirror beside the sink. They were dressed like Raggedy Ann and Andy.

"Nick, what's up, buddy?" Pecchia asked through his reptilian smile. "Want to do a little?" He pointed his thumb in at the bathroom.

"Actually, I was wondering if I could score some from you?"

"Taking Candice home, huh?"

"Thinking about it."

"That's cool. Give Candy a little blow and you can have a *good* time."

I felt a bit put off by the statement.

"Is she okay?"

"You mean is she clean?"

I just looked at him.

"As clean as anyone else you're going to meet and twice as fine."

"Yeah." I had to resign myself to the fact that risk increases exponentially with beauty.

Mark Pecchia smiled. "Let's go into my parlor," he said as he reached for the door behind me. I tried to stop him from entering the bedroom and interrupting the couple on the bed, but it was too late, he was by me in a flash. I cautiously

followed when I heard no screams. The action on the bed
never missed a beat. Pecchia didn't find anything odd about
what was happening on the pile of coats and the fuck bud-
dies didn't seem to mind the intrusion either.

"Mind if we play through, dude?" Pecchia asked the werewolf, who was still vigorously pumping away at Little Red Riding Hood.

The guy on the bed leaned up and craned his neck at us.

"No problem," he said. The guy was neither out of breath
nor embarrassed. It was like they were just doing their home-
work together.

Pecchia went around the bed to a walk-in closet. He entered the closet and rummaged about. I stood in the doorway, trying not to stare at Red and her werewolf. The girl
looked up at me. Her eyes were wide, her pupils dilated. She
was high as the proverbial kite.

"More?" she asked me innocently.

The werewolf looked up at me.

"How 'bout it, man?" he asked generously. He was absolutely the friendliest werewolf I had ever met.

I just glared at him, trying to figure it all out. There was no
answer. This guy must've thought he was back in the sixties.
Share and share alike. Mighty nice of him, but I took a pass
with a shake of my head.

Pecchia exited the closet with a small bag of coke.

"And they say this town doesn't do drugs anymore," he said.
"Hypocrites. An eight ball okay?"

"I don't need that much."

"If you're partying with Candice you do. I wish I had some
rock, but I'm all out. You'll have to cook it up yourself, if that's
what you want."

"Whatever," I said. I wasn't sure what he meant, but I

didn't want to go into it. The whole exchange was making me increasingly uncomfortable. I barely knew this guy and I was scoring coke from him. He could be a fed for all I knew. This whole party could be one big sting operation. If it was, Uncle Sam would be receiving an A for accuracy on their report card. Candice's influence had me wired. I was entering territory I usually steered away from, but I felt clearheaded and secure in my decision, as if the calculated risks were well worth the eventual results.

We started to walk out of the bedroom. "You don't have a coat in there, do you, Nick?" Pecchia asked, indicating the fuck pile with a laugh.

I shook my head negatively. We went into the hallway to do business. Pecchia handed me the coke.

"What do I owe you?" I asked.

"On the house, Nick. I owe *you*, man."

"C'mon. . . ."

"No, really, take it, enjoy."

I took the coke. What was I going to do? Argue? The guy was trying to buy in, obviously, but buy in to what? I could do nothing to help him. He could rip off all my ads he wanted for the rest of our lives and I wouldn't give a damn. Maybe he just felt generous. Or maybe he didn't want to be seen taking money for drugs. It's one thing to pass the shit out like it's Halloween candy, quite another to be making a living as a dealer. Still, if he wanted privacy we could have found someplace. He didn't seem to mind anyone seeing the exchange or hearing our conversation. It was just a simple gift between two friends. Here, bud, have some coke and then take my beautiful guest to your crib and fuck the hell out of her. Mark Pecchia was simply being a good host.

4

I entered the big room and looked around. Jennifer was making her way through the crowd in the darkened living room, obviously looking for me. A hand suddenly reached up out of nowhere, grabbed Jennifer by the arm, and pulled her down onto a couch before she could see me. Jennifer landed on top of a guy with long golden hair who must have come to the Halloween party as Fabio.

"Sammy!" she squealed.

Jennifer giggled and gave "Sammy" a great big, wet kiss. She stopped and looked at him. There was some history there. They kissed again, this time more seriously. I watched it all from the mouth of the hallway. She never knew I was there. I felt a little pang of jealousy, normal for most people, but not for me. I countered it with a sense of relief and vindication. I could go on with my plans with zero guilt. So much for the white picket fence. This was reality.

Candice sat at the bar talking to a very pretty young woman with red hair and perky tits. I could hear some of their conversation as I approached.

"If Angelo shows up, just tell him you haven't seen me. Okay?" Candice said to the redhead.

The girl waved her hand in the air in mild disgust. "Hey, it's your life," she said. She had a Texas twang that would have to go if she wanted to be anything in show biz other than a countrywestern singer.

I sidled up beside Candice.

"Ready?" I asked. I didn't want to get into a pissing match with the Texan and I sensed it could happen if I didn't move quickly.

Candice licked alcohol from her forefinger.

"Sure. Uh, Nick . . . I want you to meet my very best friend in the whole world—Patti Weigel."

I extended my hand to Patti.

"Pleased to meet you," I said. "Nick Gardner."

Patti looked at me coldly, ignoring my hand.

"Yeah. . . . Hi." She had an instant dislike for me. She knew what I was going to be doing to her friend within the hour and she wasn't happy about it. The jealousy factor was immediate and intense. This was probably not the first time this scene had been played out by these two.

Candice looked at her friend and tried to make her feel better. "Call you later, okay?"

"Whatever," Patti said, and then looked down at her drink. I couldn't tell if they were lesbians or just good friends. Not that I really cared. I would take them both on if that's what it took to get inside Candice.

Candice stood up and gave Patti a guilty kiss on the cheek.

"I love you," Candice said to her warmly.

Patti eyed me suspiciously. "Be careful," she said to Candice, not caring how I felt about it.

"Of course. Don't worry."

Candice took my arm and led me through the crowd toward the door.

"What's her problem?" I asked.

"Patti? She's just very protective of me. We're like sisters."

I looked around and saw Jennifer making out with Sammy on the couch in a far corner of the room. Zero guilt.

Candice and I stopped at the doorway.

"I've gotta get my coat," Candice said.

I thought of the two minks fucking on the coats in the back room. "Leave it," I said.

"I'll just be a minute," Candice said, then she disappeared down the hallway.

I stared out into the party. Mark Pecchia was easing his way through the crowd, patting people on the back, kissing the ladies, taking an occasional toke from a joint. The host was having a hell of a time. Pecchia stopped among a group of very severe looking Hispanic men. He seemed especially intimate with these characters, as if they had serious business together. Probably the drug connection, I figured. Among the Hispanics there stood one other Caucasian. The guy had short blond hair. He was clean cut, attractive, in his late thirties. It was subtle, but I could tell he really didn't seem happy with the company he was keeping. There was something very familiar about this guy. I knew him from somewhere, but it had to be the distant past because I couldn't quite put my finger on who he was. And then it hit me. David Rink. More than a decade older, clean shaven, but that's who it was. My old buddy, David Rink. What the fuck was he doing here at this party? What the fuck was he doing in L.A.? I figured he was long gone, but here he was, turning up like a bad penny.

Candice returned, carrying her fur coat and a large leather satchel.

"Nick?"

I snapped out of my daze. "Yeah?"

"Something wrong?"

"No," I said. "Let's go."

Candice and I turned and exited the house. As we went she said, "I think someone spilled something on my coat."

PART III

So much for safe sex.
—Nick Gardner

1

Candice and I sped along PCH in the Lamborghini. A three-quarter moon illuminated the ocean to our left. The top was still off the car, but the night was so warm that it was quite comfortable.

"You live in the Boo?" Candice asked, "the Boo" being bimbo slang for Malibu.

I nodded.

"I love the Boo," she said. "I've always wanted to live there."

"It's nice," I said. "Sometimes."

The smell of thick smoke was in the air. The Santa Ana winds were blowing soot all the way from the fires in Thousand Oaks.

"This is so romantic," Candice said. "We'll fuck while Rome burns."

I looked at her and nodded again. She laughed hysterically.

"Lighten up, honey," she said. "We're here to have a good time." With that she leaned over and unzipped my pants. Before I could protest, she had my cock in her mouth. It was immediately up and angry. She had to use all the tricks of a contortionist to get over the seat divider and gear shift but it didn't seem to impede her skill as a fellationist. She was impeccable. I had to concentrate to keep the car on the road as she licked and sucked away. I didn't want a repeat of what had happened on Sunset Boulevard with Jennifer.

I reached down into Candice's top with my free hand and fondled one of her firm, round breasts. They were real. No silicone or saline here. I didn't want to come at this time, but she wasn't going to allow any such resistance. She hit some rhythms that I'd never quite felt before and suddenly I was spurting into her mouth. Unlike Jennifer who splattered my car and my clothes earlier in the day, Candice swallowed every drop thus protecting the finish of the upholstery and reducing my dry cleaning bill. I was greatly indebted to her and planned on finding a way to repay her as soon as possible.

Candice sat up and pretended to gargle before swallowing with a laugh. She was getting a big kick out of her sexual abandon.

I hit the remote for my garage door and Candice gave a silent nod of approval as she saw our destination. She obviously had a penchant for beach property.

Candice and I entered my darkened house. I turned on a small lamp in the living room. Then my stereo. An old tune by the Eagles filled the room. Candice went to the couch and sat down. She placed the leather satchel on the deco coffee table in front of her and started sifting through it, bringing out various items of freebasing paraphernalia and lining them up on the table in front of her. She had it all. A bong, a mini-blowtorch, razor blades, ether, "the works" as they say. I felt a little pang of nausea at the sight of it all. This girl was turning out to be a classic coke whore.

"Looks like you've got a whole drugstore in there," I said.

"Everything but," Candice replied, staring at me hungrily. I stared back at her for a moment until I realized what she meant. She didn't want me. She wanted the coke. Now!

"Uh, oh, yeah . . . right, here," I stammered. I pulled the bag of coke out from under my jacket and handed it to her. She immediately dumped the contents out on the table and started separating the white powder into tidy lines of equal proportion.

I nervously pulled out a cigarette and walked over to a sitting table. I grabbed a book of matches and discovered they were all used up.

"Got a light?" I asked.

Candice fired up her mini-blowtorch. It created an intense flame that I did not want to get very close to.

"How about matches?" I asked.

Candice frowned, killed the torch, and handed me a bright red butane lighter. There was lettering on the outside of the lighter that read "The Eight Ball." Underneath the lettering there was a fancy design of an eight ball. I almost asked Candice where the lighter had come from, then I decided I didn't want to know. I was quickly realizing that the less I knew about this woman's life, the better I was going to feel. If she had not been so drop-dead gorgeous I would have called for a taxi and sent her on her way. But she was too hot and I was too horny and stupid to follow my better instincts.

I lit my cigarette and watched as Candice precooked the coke-ether mixture. After a few minutes of diligent chemistry, Candice loaded up the bong with hardened coke, then fired it all up with the minitorch. She took a hit, leaned back, and let the drug take over. A few moments later she exhaled and began twitching from the rush.

"Oh yes," she moaned with pleasure.

After a long period of silent reverie, Candice offered the bong to me.

"I don't base," I said.

"Heeey," Candice squealed. "I thought this was going to be a celebration?"

I got up off the couch and crossed to the small wet bar on the far side of the room.

"It is. I just don't do coke. Haven't in a long time." I poured myself a tall Jack Daniel's and dropped in a few ice cubes from the minifridge behind the bar.

"Sort of a personal code, eh?" Candice said.

"You could say that. I had some problems with it a long time ago."

I returned with my drink. Candice began to cook some more coke. "Well, if you really want to party with Candy, you've got to do as Candy does."

I sat down on the sofa opposite her.

"Why?"

"So I don't feel like I'm doing anything wrong."

"It's nothing personal. I just don't do coke."

"You just supply it, right?" An edge of bitterness was creeping into her voice.

"Look, you asked for the stuff. I got it for you. What more do you want?"

Candice looked at me for a long, uncomfortable moment.

"Nothing, Nick. You got your blow job. What more do *you* want?"

I eased back into the sofa, trying to regain my composure.

"I think we're getting off on the wrong foot. I thought we were going to have a nice, low-key evening together. . . ."

"And then at the end of the evening you planned on fucking my brains out. Or did I read you wrong?" Candice fired up the bong.

I stared at her for a bit before responding.

"No. You didn't read me wrong."

Candice took a quick hit and let it wash over her for a few seconds. Then she stood up, wanting to illustrate her moral high ground. She was a little wobbly on her feet.

"Then why wait till the end of the evening?"

She undid her belt and let it drop to the floor. She pulled her shirt over her head, revealing she was totally naked underneath. She wasn't even wearing G-string panties. I took it all in, saying nothing. Her body was as beautiful as I had imagined. A perfect female specimen. As long as she wasn't talking. Or freebasing. She was a living, breathing centerfold sans staples. The kind of creature that young boys fantasized about in the privacy of bathrooms and wealthy old men wept over while writing rent checks.

Candice stepped around the table and stood in front of me. She bent forward and took my zipper between her thumb and index finger. She pulled it straight out, then methodically started to pull the zipper down. She went slow this time. Very ritualistic. We had all night.

Candice bent forward and kissed me on the lips. I remained perfectly still, but did nothing to resist her. She worked her lips along my neck, down my chest, pulling open my shirt as she went, over my stomach, then she buried her head in my lap for the second time that night.

I leaned my head back and reveled in the sensation. I shifted and slid my pants down around my ankles. I wanted to be inside her. Candice read my mind. She climbed up onto the couch and lowered herself down onto me, engulfing my cock with her hot flesh. She had trimmed her pubic hair to the bare minimum without actually getting out a razor. There was not a nanosecond of unwanted resistance or entanglement as I slid deep inside her. It was a perfect fit. Condoms were never even mentioned. So much for safe sex.

Candice slowly rocked back and forth, sliding me in and out over and over again. Once she had scoped out the territory and estimated my limitations she picked up the tempo and began pumping away with total precision. She knew to a fraction of an inch just how far she could move without interrupting service. I reached around and grabbed the cheeks of her round ass, kneading them, separating them, squeezing them together, pulling them apart. She was firm, but still fleshy enough to be fun.

We rolled to the floor, never missing a beat. The ocean kept time for us just outside the windows.

Candice seemed to be straining, but not as if she was having a great time. It was more like she was *trying* to enjoy herself. As if she wasn't getting what she needed out of the experience, but wanted it desperately. She reached behind herself, grabbed my balls, and tried to shove them up into her along with my cock. She jerked and jumped as certain spots were touched that gave her pleasure. She grabbed the base of my cock and pulled on it until I came, once again involuntarily, but intensely, inside of her. She leaned forward and took a long breath, then climbed off of me and headed for her bong again.

She lit the thing and took another drag off of it. I'd seen people freebase before, but I'd never seen anyone with this kind of tolerance. Usually a good hit would knock the smoker on his or her ass for twenty minutes or so. Not this one. She had built up an immunity. She'd fade for a couple of minutes after a hit, but she would snap back like nothing had happened soon afterward.

I was still on the floor, exhausted, watching Candice float into the netherworld. I got up, went to the bar, and made another drink. If she was going to be fucked up I wanted a good buzz myself to make it all palatable. I stood at the bar, sipping my drink and watching her naked body sway to the rhythms of the late-night music coming from KTYD, a Santa Barbara radio station that I could just barely receive because of my location on the beach. If I had been a mile inland I wouldn't have been able to pick it up at all. I liked their stuff. The station catered to a college beach town and I found the selections refreshing. A good blend of oldies and new rock with an edge. They were playing an Eric Clapton piece from one of the albums he recorded a few years before his son went out a window and his sainthood had become complete.

Candice was beginning to drip a little on the couch. It was time to move the action into the bedroom. Or out the front door, whichever she preferred.

After a few minutes Candice came around. She cleaned the bowl and began to pack fresh coke into it. I couldn't believe it.

"Haven't you had enough?" I asked.

Candice turned and looked over her shoulder at me seductively. "Enough of what?"

She knew what I meant and I could tell what she meant. I was talking drugs, she was trying to throw me off with more sex. I answered directly anyway.

"Enough coke."

"I never get enough of anything. That's my problem. I'm insatiable."

She fired the bong and took a small hit. Her eyes were glassy. I brought my drink over and sat down on the couch next to her.

"Mark Pecchia warned me about you," I said.

She looked hurt, as if something dark had suddenly been revealed about her without being actually articulated. She leaned forward so I couldn't watch her face.

"He did?" Her voice cracked a little.

"It wasn't really a warning. He just said that you liked to have a good time."

Candice turned and looked at me. She seemed to regain a bit of confidence and there was spite in her voice.

"Who doesn't?" she asked. It was more of an accusation than a question.

I relaxed into the soft couch and studied Candice's lovely body and ugly addiction. She grabbed a cigarette, got up, walked to the window, and looked out at the moonlit ocean. Her hands vibrated as she fired up the smoke. She looked at me and winced.

"You guys are all the same. You use whatever you can to get what you want and you just don't give a fuck about anything else. . . . You sit there with a drink in one hand and your dick in the other and you think you can judge me, judge *my* problems."

"I'm not judging you."

"Bullshit! You fuck the hell out of me on the floor of your little beach house in the Boo, then look down on me because I like to party. . . . You didn't even try to make me come!"

I looked at her hard. I didn't know whether I should be angry or embarrassed. I was a little of both.

"I thought you *did* come," I said.

"It'll take more than what you've got to get me off."

I got up and approached her. She was pushing my buttons.

"Look, lady, I don't know what kind of trip you're on, but I'm getting pretty sick of your shit. Just what the hell do you want out of me?"

Candice radically softened. She was going through changes quickly. She said, "I want you to reach me."

Candice lowered her cigarette and touched it to her skin right above her pubic area. The smell of burnt hair and flesh wafted into the air. I was momentarily stunned, then I reached out and knocked the cigarette out of her hand, onto the floor. I stomped out the butt with my bare foot, burning myself in the process.

"Goddamnit!" I yelled, rubbing the bottom of my foot.

"Like it?" Candice asked.

I was disgusted. I walked away from her.

"I think it's time for you to go home," I said.

"All done with me?"

"Yeah. We're finished."

I tossed Candice her shirt. She made no move to catch it and it fell to the floor.

"I can't go yet."

"I insist."

"Please let me stay with you. Just for tonight."

The girl was totally schizo. I approached her again and looked into her eyes. Her pupils were big and round.

"I'm not into these kinds of games," I said.

"I know lots of others." She bit her bottom lip with imagination suddenly run amok.

"I'm not interested."

She reached out and put her arms around my neck.

"Don't make me go . . . not yet."

She bent her head and nuzzled under my chin so that she

didn't have to look at me directly. She was about to beg and
what little dignity she had left resisted eye contact.

"I could do things for you, Nick. Things your other girls
won't do."

"Like drive me crazy?"

"Whatever you want, I'll do. However you want me, I'll be.
Use me up, Nick. Use me all night long."

Her left hand trailed down my body, searching. When she
found what she wanted she squeezed it gently. I immediately
began to get hard again.

"I belong to you tonight," she continued. "I'm your property. Fuck me. Kill me. . . ."

"Just don't make you write bad checks, right?"

"Just don't send me away."

She moaned and began moving her hand gently, rhythmically. I was torn between the reality that this woman was nuts
and the fact that my cock was hard as a rock again. I split the
difference and led her upstairs to the bedroom.

PART IV

Tie me up. I know it's a little old-fashioned, but I like it.
—Candice Bishop

1

The room was dark, lit only by the illumination from a large aquarium against one wall. The aquarium was filled with large black angelfish. No other color escaped the tank save for the white gravel on the bottom. Even the plants were black. I like things simple. Even my fish.

I lowered Candice onto the bed. We wrestled for a while in what the natives refer to as the missionary position. Candice was responding more than she did downstairs but there was still something forced about her appearance. She finally gave a moan and straightened her legs spasmodically, signaling that I had at last fulfilled my part of the bargain. I drove into her a few more times and came again myself. I shook her at the end of my cock like a lion would shake a dead antelope. Once I felt completely drained I relaxed on top of her. She lay staring up at the ceiling for a few minutes, lost in some late-hour half dream, then she slid out from under me and went downstairs to get her works.

She brought it all upstairs and began cleaning and loading the bong again. She stacked her paraphernalia neatly on a nightstand next to the bed. I sat up and lighted a cigarette. It was going to be a long night.

"Have you ever freebased?" Candice asked.

"No."

I felt embarrassed, as if never freebasing had left me out of some elite club. I'd done my share of drugs in the last twenty years, but freebasing was beyond my need for experience. I'd seen too many people total their lives at the end of that pipe.

"But you have done coke, haven't you?"

"Of course."

"Of course," she mocked.

Candice lit the bong and took a small toke. She held it before exhaling. She was a seasoned pro at this game. I suddenly realized that her orgasm a few minutes ago was just an act to get me off and, subsequently, off of her, so she could go down and get her drugs.

"You still haven't come, have you?" I asked.

She responded as if the answer was obvious and I was silly for asking it. "I can't come with someone who isn't as high as I am."

"Bullshit."

"No. I'm serious. It's weird, but when I'm high, I just can't come with someone who isn't."

I got out of bed and stood in front of Candice. My penis brushed her forehead. She brushed it back playfully.

"You are a deeply disturbed young woman," I said.

Candice laughed. "You've disturbed me pretty deeply tonight, that's for sure. Tell me you haven't liked it."

"I haven't liked it," I said halfheartedly. I knelt down between her legs and kissed her thighs, working my way up her body. She saw right through me.

"You're a liar."

"I want you to come," I said.

Candice leaned back on the bed and let my tongue find her.

"Then get high with me," she said. She positioned her legs wider to get more comfortable. I licked her like a cat lapping up cream.

"Really, this is nice," she said between breaths, "but I want to see you smoke."

She grabbed me by the hair, pulled my head out of her lap and looked me in the face. "Smoke some with me, then I'll give you something I bet you haven't had in a long time."

"I told you I don't freebase."

"Then don't complain about not reaching me." She closed her legs on me as if she was taking a toy away from a bad child.

I stood up again. This was getting ridiculous.

"I think you're totally fucked, but if it means that much to you, I'll take a hit."

I pulled up a chair and sat in front of Candice.

"A couple of hits," Candice insisted. "You won't get it with just one."

"A couple of hits. Then you'll be happy?"

"Then we'll be equals."

"We're equals now."

"No we're not. You have to reach my level before you can fully possess me. I can't feel anything until we're on the same plane." Candice lit the bong and offered it to me.

I looked at the bong for a long time before accepting it. Finally, I took a hit.

Candice decided to coach me through it like I was having a baby via Lamaze. "Hold it. . . . Hold it. . . . Okay. . . . Let it out."

I exhaled. The high hit me like a cold wave. My face

flushed and the room spun around me. She had lied. One hit was *more* than enough to fuck me up. Candice took the bong, took another hit, then sat the bong on the nightstand.

"Feel it?" she asked.

It seemed like a lifetime before I could speak. It was probably only a few seconds.

"Yeah. I think I'm on the plane to your level. . . . Meet me at the gate," I babbled like a drunken idiot, trying to make light of my desperate condition.

Candice slid up onto the bed and spread her legs wide.

"This is your gate. Come and get it."

I crawled on top of Candice and began kissing her neck and shoulders. My eyes were glassy from the booze and the coke. I felt light as a feather.

"Nick, there's something I want you to do . . . to get us even closer."

"Anything."

"Tie me up."

"What?"

"Tie me up. I know it's a little old-fashioned, but I like it."

"I don't have any rope."

"You've got neckties, don't you?"

"Sure."

"Well, *get* them."

I went to my closet and grabbed a bunch of silk ties off my tie rack. I clumsily tied Candice's foot to a bedpost. She was lying on her stomach. I pulled her legs apart and tied her other foot to the other bedpost. I repeated the procedure with her hands, tying each to opposing bedposts at the head of the bed. The bed frame was made of wrought iron, but I had never strapped anyone to it before. I could only hope that the welds would hold during the following stress test.

I looked at Candice like that for a long time, bound and exposed, totally vulnerable to whatever I might want to do to her. The longer I looked, the more she squirmed. The suspense was driving her crazy.

"C'mon, Nick. Don't just stand there. Fuck me!"

"I'm still thinking about it."

She began flailing on the bed, thrusting her hips into the air hungrily. The flailing turned into thrashing. I thought she was going to either hurt herself or destroy my bed. I waited until she thoroughly exhausted herself. She collapsed onto the mattress like a broken bronco. It appeared to be a safe time to approach.

I crawled on top of Candice and entered her from behind. She gasped with satisfaction. I slowly, rhythmically pumped away. Candice finally seemed to be feeling something, but it was an even more intense experience for me. My face was straining, veins popping out all over, sweat pouring down my brow. But Candice needed to go further.

"You know where I want it," she said.

I was shocked. It had been a wild night so far, but I hadn't had a request like that since the seventies. We were already rolling the dice big time by not using condoms. Now she wanted it in the ass. I was caught in a fever of drugs and lust and now there was nothing I wanted more than to comply with this gorgeous coke whore.

Candice's face contorted with a mixture of pleasure, relief, and agony as I repositioned myself and entered the forbidden territory. We were both so slick with sex that artificial lubrication was unnecessary. I got on my knees, moving gently behind her, guiding her ass cheeks with my hands. She began to twist and turn her head, wanting a kiss. I leaned forward and complied and she bit me on the ear as I started to pull away.

"Harder, Nick, harder!" she commanded.

I was already raw to the bone, but I picked up the pace like a good stud. She was freaking out.

"Fuck me, Nick! Fuck me. . . . I hate you . . . I hate you . . . mother*fucker!*"

I was really banging away now, pulling her ass upwards against my groin with both hands. Passion turned to hate, hate turned to lust, lust turned to some sort of existential agony that neither of us could comprehend. Nothing was going to completely satisfy us now unless we could actually molecularly bond and become one animal, one engine that would continue fucking itself into the next century.

Candice strained at her bonds, shaking my bed to the point it almost broke apart. Tears streamed down her face.

"Fuck me, fuck me harder, you bastard!" she screamed.

I reached under Candice and manipulated her clitoris with my right hand, occasionally delving up into her steaming vagina. She was soaking wet.

"*Yes . . . yes . . . I'm coming!*" she screamed. "*Come with me! Come with me, baby! Tear me up!*"

Candice pushed her hips up against me as hard as she could with the bonds restraining her. I pounded away until we both stiffened up in the most intense shared orgasm I've ever experienced. Hot fluids poured out of her as I pinched and stroked her rigid clitoris. It twitched under my touch. I didn't think I could come again, but I did. She drained every last drop of semen from my body.

I collapsed on top of Candice's back, totally exhausted. I was breathing hard now, blood pressure 220 over 165. I was definitely done for the night. Maybe for the rest of my life. Candice was another matter altogether.

"Don't stop now, Nick," she said. "We're so close. . . ."

I was shocked.

"You still didn't come?"

"Sure I did, but we could go further, tonight. We could go all the way."

What the hell did that mean?

"I can't do any more," I said.

"Yes you can. I'll help you."

She shook her hair out of her face, looked over her shoulder, and said, "Put it in my mouth, Nick."

I lifted up off of her, amazed. She hadn't lied about her sex drive. She *was* insatiable and she *would* do anything. I stared at her hungry, waiting mouth for a moment, then slid out of her and started to move forward.

PART V

You should get laid more often.

—Lou Collins

1

Sunlight streamed through the venetian blinds into the bedroom. I could feel the sun, but I still couldn't fully wake up. I had suffered a workout that would last awhile and the drugs and booze had not helped matters.

The phone rang. I jolted upright for a moment, then collapsed back into bed. I looked around the room. It was spinning slowly, rotating, lifting at the corners over and over again as if the whole place was going to capsize. Candice was gone, but the silk ties still dangled from the metal bedposts, mute testament to the debauchery that had occurred only hours earlier.

I hung my head over the side of the bed. It was going to be a rough day in Hangover City. I slowly slid off the bed onto the floor and lay there, staring up at the ceiling. The phone continued to ring, an impossible six feet away, high up on the nightstand.

I reached out, grabbed the telephone cord, and pulled the phone off the nightstand just in time to keep the answering machine from picking up. I dragged the thing toward me and put the receiver to my ear.

"Yeah?"

It was Lou.

"Nick, where the fuck are you?" he growled.

I looked around the room, thinking about the stupidity of the question.

"Here," I said.

"Yeah, well, you're supposed to be *here*, partner. We got six models lined up collecting paychecks."

"What time is it?"

"Ten-twenty-six exactly. . . . You're late. Way late. Again!"

Lou was getting fed up with my behavioral patterns. I felt like hanging up on him—let him shoot his own fucking pictures—but I resisted the impulse.

"Shit. . . . I'll be right in," I groaned.

"You're fucked up, aren't you?" Lou was a master of understatement.

"Don't worry about it. I'll be fine."

"I'll send a driver over."

"Forget it, I said I'm fine."

"You don't sound fine. Get a shower and be ready in half an hour."

I acquiesced. "Yeah," I coughed into the receiver before hanging up.

I lay on the floor a few more moments, then struggled into a crawling position. I slithered over to the bedroom window and climbed up the wall until I was on my feet.

I stood with one hand on either side of the window holding myself steady, trying not to throw up. I looked around the room and had a vague memory of the girl who was there a few hours earlier. I was glad she was gone. Better yet, I was glad to still be alive. My bones ached and my head felt like it was going to burst. My groin looked like it had bounced off a land mine, but I was still breathing.

I stared out through the window into the sunlit street below. Cars zoomed by on the Pacific Coast Highway. A grizzled-looking homeless guy strolled along the street with his shopping cart looking for valuable Malibu discards. The PC crowd insists we call these people "homeless" or "disenfranchised" or "dislocated." It gives all concerned a feeling of respect, but the fact was this guy was just a plain, old-fashioned bum. A character who felt more at home sleeping on the beach than confined within the four walls of society's norm. As I stared at the man I realized that he bore more than a passing resemblance to me. We could be cousins if not brothers. I stared down at the bum, then felt my own unshaven face. There but for the grace of whatever. And then again, maybe not.

I looked over at the bed, then around the room. A battlefield without honor. I shook my head slowly, took one more look out the window at the bum, then staggered to the bathroom to try to prepare for the day.

2

After showering and dressing, I looked out my window at the street below. A long, dark limo sat in front of my house. Steve, the limo driver, sat behind the wheel reading a *Penthouse* magazine. The limo service sent Steve whenever they could. He had the proper temperament to tolerate my lifestyle.

The bum was still working the neighborhood. He was very methodical. He was now rummaging through one of two large green Dumpsters between my house and my neighbor's place.

I exited the house, carrying some gear. I looked better. Not good, just better. I still felt like shit. I had eaten some Tylenol and a few vitamins when I first went into the bathroom, but I puked them up in the middle of my shower.

Steve dropped his magazine, jumped out of the car, and ran around to the other side to open my door for me. This was a move that always embarrassed me.

"How many times have I told you not to do that, Steve?"

"Sorry, Mr. Gardner. It's instinct."

"Call me Nick."

"Yes, sir."

I stared at him for a moment, irritated that he didn't get it, then said, "I'll ride in front with you."

I opened the front passenger-side door and climbed in. Steve walked around to his side of the car and got in, tossing the *Penthouse* in my direction.

The bum was up in the Dumpster now, prodding the trash with a bent metal pole, looking for valuables. The pole struck something deep within the Dumpster. He fished around and pulled up some new treasure with the homemade divining rod. It was a green plastic trash bag dripping some kind of dark fluid, oil, maybe blood. It looked like someone had thrown away some bad meat. I almost vomited again thinking about it. Luckily Steve pulled away and the sight was replaced by a bright sunny day at the beach.

We drove to the studio in total silence. I wasn't up to any form of conversation. At one point I picked up the *Penthouse* magazine, then quickly dropped it back on the seat. Even the vision of beautiful naked women nauseated me.

I wanted sunshine and caffeine. I got plenty of sunshine on the drive into town. The caffeine could wait until my stomach quit boiling.

3

The set was a continuation of the Collision design from the day before, only now one of the cars was upside down on top of the other car. It was Salvatore's idea, of course, and it looked great. Luckily the car bodies we had rented were only shells, so with the proper rigging little, if any, damage was done. The same models from the previous day's shoot were back. They were lounging around off to the side awaiting my arrival. They had a lot in common with the cars. All look, not a lot happening under the hood. I came in quietly through the back door and scanned the scene to see how tense the situation had become.

Jennifer was standing near the phones, talking with Lou. They didn't notice my arrival.

"Fucking guy," Lou said. "I hope he's not going to go through another one of his 'difficult' periods."

"I saw what he went home with last night," Jennifer snapped. "He may be sore for a few days, but I think he'll get over it."

"Good." Lou was always the pragmatist.

I stepped out of the shadows and they both looked guilty. *How much did he hear?*

"Finally," Lou said, trying to cover for himself.

"Sorry," I said, not meaning it for a second.

"How you feeling?" Lou asked, putting on his best fatherly voice.

Jennifer stared flame at me. I returned a blank gaze at her as I answered Lou, "Fine. Let's do it."

I walked the set for a few minutes, gave instructions to the crew, then sat down in my tall director's chair. My legs were like spaghetti. Whitney brought me three extrastrength Tylenol and some bottled water.

"A little Kate Bush today, boss?" Whitney asked. Kate Bush was de rigueur around here when I had a hangover. Her music and voice were hot enough to get everyone's juices flowing without making me scream. There was something soothing about her primordial wails that usually gave me reason to live before the day was over.

"Let her loose," I said to Whitney. He scurried off to the sound system.

I gave simple instructions to the models and then the music came. It was one of my favorites, "Rocket's Tail." I smiled and said, "Places everyone."

I had Jennifer decked out in her sultry cop outfit, doing suggestive things to the two "driver" models with her handcuffs, nightstick, and pistol while three of the atmosphere models played sexy shocked bystanders in the background. I shot furiously. I was getting great stuff. Jennifer was very angry at me and it was showing through in just the way I wanted. She looked like she could snap at any moment and actually start opening fire with her weapon.

———

Anyone can squeeze you into a negli-nothing and slap some makeup on you and get a look, but Nicky will capture your hidden kinks, your darkest desires.

—Jennifer Joyner

———

Lou and a handful of ad agency goofs stood off to the side near the crew, watching the action. After the previous day's fiasco I guess confidence in my work had slipped a notch or two. Lou seemed pleased with the way things were going now.

We went three straight, hot hours without a break. I wanted to get as much of it as I could while it was working. We were all about to drop by the time I clicked off my last series of shots. The models were soaked with sweat.

"That's it," I said. "We're done."

Everyone relaxed on the set. Collapsed would be a better word. I dropped my arms to my sides and stared at the models for a few moments.

The crew and the ad agency guys suddenly burst into applause, led by Lou, who was quite jubilant. He stepped onto the set and slapped me on the back. Then he led me off to the side.

"You should get laid more often," he said. "That was fucking great. I don't know what you said to Jennifer, but she was hot! The Collision people are very impressed." Lou pointed at the ad guys. A pack of horny dogs who were now moving in on the models.

I was very tired. Not just because of the night before or even what we had just done. I was tired of the whole scene. Even of Lou. It was all getting very stale.

"We're gonna get a lot of action off this campaign," Lou bubbled, irritating me even more.

"Yeah," I muttered.

"You must be beat," Lou said. "Want to do a couple of lines in my office?"

"You know me better than that. I'm going home."

"Okay. Get some rest. We've got that lipstick thing to do on Monday."

"Right."

Lou slapped me on the back again. "Rare form today, buddy. Rare form."

Lou moved off, targeting in on one of the female atmosphere models. He connected with her like a heat-seeking
missile. I watched them talk for a moment before Jennifer got
to me.

"So, how was it?" she asked, wiping sweat from her face
with a towel.

"You were great," I said.

"I meant *last night.*"

I didn't feel like putting up with any badgering.

"That was great too. How was it for you?"

"You bastard. You don't give an inch, do you?"

"Problem with you, Jenn, someone gives you an inch, you
want ten more."

Jennifer hit me in the face with her towel and spit, "Fuck
you!" at me in her most hostile hiss. Then she turned and
stormed off toward the dressing rooms.

I felt the red area that the towel left on my face and I smiled.

———

*Settle down with Nick? No way. He'd just as soon fuck
the maid of honor as cut the cake. He'd bang the entire
catering staff while they were making hors d'oeuvres.
He's a satyr, pure and simple. A great fuck, but a shitty
lover. Love is forbidden in his world. Me, I believe in love.
I just don't believe it exists within the L.A. county line.*

—Jennifer Joyner

———

PART VI

That's a new one, huh?

—Edgar Thompson

1

Steve had read his *Penthouse* cover to cover by the time I got out of the studio. I sat in the front seat of the limo again, watching the traffic. It was a lot easier to take when you weren't behind the wheel. I was feeling a little better. My internal organs were finally shifting into their proper places. We hit PCH just as the sun was beginning to set. I looked at Steve and wondered why he was a limo driver. He seemed smart and physically capable. There were plenty of other jobs he could be doing that would pay better and offer more reward. I fired up a cigarette and rolled the window down so I wouldn't smoke him out.

"Ever think of doing anything else?" I asked.

"You mean instead of driving?"

I nodded.

"Not for a few years now. When I first came to L.A. I wanted to be a movie director. Graduated USC, even spent a year at the American Film Institute."

"So, what happened?"

"I drive limos now."

I stared at him for a moment. That answer said it all; another L.A. casualty settling for the grim reality of paying the bills over the dream that had brought him out to the West Coast. It was amazing how many stayed in Los Angeles long after the dream was over. The city is like a terrible drug. Addictive in the worst way. Everyone hates it, yet most of them stay no matter what the cost. Some manage to leave, only to return a year or so later. Very few have the intestinal fortitude to kick the insanity for good and live elsewhere. The dream is always there, a brass ring only inches outside their reach. Can't get the ring if you're not on the ride.

I turned my attention back to the road to keep from embarrassing Steve any further. I could see my house up ahead. An ambulance and a number of police cars, marked and unmarked, were parked around the strip of houses surrounding mine and a small crowd of onlookers had gathered behind barricades. Reporters were everywhere, like a swarm of hungry insects.

"Looks like trouble," Steve said.

"My neighbor has probably been beating his wife again. Don't ever live next door to actors."

Steve laughed. "I know what you mean," he said. "When I first got to L.A. I lived under one of the Baldwin's. . . . I never got any sleep."

Steve pulled up as close to my driveway as he could get without breaking a barricade. He opened the door and ran around to my side. I got out before he could get there.

"It's okay, Steve. I've got it."

I looked over at my house. Police were walking in and out of my front door.

"They're in *your* house, Mr. Gardner."

"I can see that." I slipped Steve a twenty, patted him on the shoulder, and started walking toward the house.

"You want me to stick around?" Steve asked.

"No. Go on. I'll be fine."

I walked up the stairs and entered the front door, which was standing open. A patrolman stopped me at the doorway. "I'm sorry, you can't come in here," he said politely, yet sternly.

"This is *my* house."

The patrolman was suddenly very excited. "Are you Nick Gardner?"

"Yes."

"Come with me, sir."

I followed the patrolman up the stairs to the second floor. A complete forensic team was at work in the master bedroom. The activity was rotating around two men; a short, prematurely gray man who was dressed like he was ready to go to a wedding, and a much taller, handsome man in his early thirties who looked quite a bit more casual. The short man was obviously in charge of whatever was going on and the younger, taller man was his flunky. Business was revolving around the short man's instructions, which were brisk and calm. He had a quiet air of authority, like the whole affair, whatever it was, had already been figured out and he was just mopping up, doing the paperwork. The patrolman accompanying me seemed almost afraid to interrupt him.

"Lieutenant Di Bacco," he said from across the room.

The two men turned and saw us. The short man motioned for the taller man to approach us while he finished what he was working on. The tall man strode over, already putting a name to my face.

"Nick Gardner?" the tall man asked firmly.

"Yes," I said. "What's this all about?"

The tall man looked over at the short man and nodded. Then he turned back to me and said, "Just a moment, please."

The short man came over and faced me. He had beady eyes, more suited to a criminal than a cop. Sometimes it's just a flip of the coin.

"Nick Gardner?" His voice was deep and rough, like some cop on prime time television.

"That's right. For the third time, I'm Nick Gardner."

"That's very good," Di Bacco said. "I'm Lieutenant Archibald Di Bacco, Sheriff's Department, Homicide Division. This is my partner, Detective Sergeant Edgar Thompson. It is our duty to inform you that you are under arrest for possession of controlled substances and suspicion of murder."

A nausea of confusion and fear began to knot in my stomach.

"What?" It was the best I could come up with at the moment.

Thompson showed me a piece of paper on a clipboard. "This is a warrant to search your premises," he said. "Under this warrant we are mandated to arrest you if we find incriminating evidence. This evidence is in abundance."

"What the fuck are you talking about?" I asked.

Thompson looked at the patrolman and said, "Cuff him."

The patrolman grabbed my arms and cuffed them behind my back before I could even respond. Then Thompson began reading me my rights. Di Bacco turned and walked back toward the bed.

"There's something wrong here," I said. "You've got the wrong person! I didn't kill anybody! What the hell are you try-

ing to do to me? I want to call my attorneys. Someone listen
to me for God's sake! I'm talking to you!"

No one in the room responded to my pleas. Thompson finished reading my rights. "Have you understood everything I
have said to you?" he asked.

I hadn't heard a word, but I said yes automatically. He
wasn't speaking Swahili. The patrolman took me by the back
of the neck and started to lead me down the stairs. I tried to
resist, but the cop held firm, forcing me forward. I tried to
get Di Bacco's attention.

"Will someone please listen to me? I'm telling you you're
making a big mistake!" They ignored me as I was forced down
the stairwell. I could hear Thompson and Di Bacco laugh as
they disappeared from my view.

"That's a new one, huh?" Thompson said.

We were joined by a second patrolman downstairs.

"This the guy?" the new arrival asked.

The first patrolman nodded and grunted. The second patrolman looked at me like I was the lowest form of slime on
the planet and shook his head slowly. They led me out of the
house and toward a black and white police car. I wasn't re-
sisting anymore, but my pressure cooker was working over-
time.

The reporters surrounded us like hungry jackals. Video
cameras whirred and shutters clicked like machine gun fire.
The cacophony of questions that flew at us blended into one
loud rushing stream. I could feel the blood boiling in my
head. I wanted to be anywhere other than here.

As the cops put me into the backseat of the patrol car, I
looked across the way to the large Dumpsters that the bum
had been rummaging through when I left the house earlier

in the day. More forensic men were at work there. Yellow
plastic bags of varying sizes and shapes were being pho-
tographed on the ground next to the Dumpster. Blood was
visible on most of the bags. My worst fears were beginning
to take tangible form. Someone had been killed and somehow I was getting the blame.

The homeless guy was sitting in a chair off to the side, sipping coffee from a Styrofoam cup. A lady cop stood over him.
He looked happy. This was his moment in the sun, the re-
mainder of the fifteen minutes of fame that Andy Warhol had
promised him. Whatever he had logged in before he took the
streets as a residence was about to be eclipsed. This was better than winning the high school football game or taking a
shell for a buddy in Vietnam and getting the Purple Heart and
a twelve-line story in the local paper. He had discovered the
key evidence in a murder investigation. The grisly remains of
a body, chopped up and wrapped neatly in plastic and loaded
into my Dumpster. Well, that wouldn't be enough to get me
in trouble. The cops were making a big mistake. You can't just
arrest someone for having a body in his Dumpster. The thing
was in plain sight on the Pacific Coast Highway. The public
has access to it. There was no way they could realistically connect me to whoever was in those plastic bags. After a few
hours I would be free and clear and ready to prepare a lawsuit for false arrest.

The cops got into the front seat of the patrol car and we
pulled away. I craned my neck to see my house, trying to figure out just exactly what had happened. My garage door was
open now. More cops were surrounding my Lamborghini.
They were laughing it up, having a good old time. Guys like
that love to see guys like me get their dicks caught in a

wringer. But I'd have the last laugh, once my attorneys got on the case.

Steve, the chauffeur, was still there. Two cops were asking him questions. I wondered if I would still be a favorite customer next time I saw him.

As my house faded from view in the distance, I began to feel more confident, almost cocky. This was such a huge mistake that I almost felt sorry for the Sheriff's Department. There would be a big lawsuit once I unraveled this mess. I looked at the two cops in the front seat of the car. They were stoic and bored already.

"Anyone mind telling me who I supposedly killed?" I asked.

The driver replied without emotion, without even looking into the rearview mirror.

"Candice Bishop."

2

I sat across a table from Lieutenant Di Bacco in a windowless twelve-by-fifteen-foot interrogation room. A large mirror filled one wall. It was obviously two-way glass with a video camera mounted on the other side in a room where everyone could get together and watch the worms squirm. Two other detectives in disheveled suits stood off to the side watching Di Bacco work. Thompson was not in the room. I presumed he was on the other side of the mirror.

I was beat. We'd been at it awhile.

"Might as well make a clean slate of it, Gardner," Di Bacco said, for what seemed to be the hundredth time. "We have a dozen witnesses that say you left the party with the girl last night. Her prints were all over your house. *Both* your prints were on narcotics paraphernalia found beside your bed. You even had half a gram of cocaine left on your dresser. There was evidence of recent sexual activity in the room. Your semen matched the semen found in her body, which was conveniently located in the Dumpster outside your house, along with the machete used to kill her."

I scratched my arm nervously. It looked bad, no doubt about it.

"You're in a lot of trouble, Mr. Gardner," Di Bacco continued. "Why don't you save us all a shitload of time and aggravation and just come clean?"

I looked at him with total frustration. "I've been telling you all night: I didn't do it. I was with her last night, yeah, but I didn't kill her. I didn't even *know* the girl."

"You knew her well enough to freebase with her," Di Bacco said. "You knew her well enough to have sex with her. I think you knew her well enough to kill her."

"Look, I met the girl at the party last night, she was beautiful, she came on to me. Tell me *you* wouldn't have taken her home."

"I don't think my wife would have approved."

"Yeah, well, I don't have a wife."

A clerk entered the room and handed a thick manila file to Di Bacco, then exited. Di Bacco began reading the file. Finally he looked up at me and grinned in a very satisfied way that made me feel queasy.

"You may not be married, but you're about to enter a long-term relationship with the state of California, Mr. *Bracken.*"

I looked at Di Bacco with a level of horror that made my more recent expressions of shock seem tame. Di Bacco flipped a page in the file and began reading out loud.

"Nicholas Bracken, also known as Nick Gardner, charged with conspiracy to pander in 1981 and 1983—"

"I can explain that," I protested.

"Then you left the States in '86. We don't know where you were until you filed for an official name change from London in 1990. You came to New York in '92 and moved back to L.A. a year later. You've been running from something, Nick. And guess what? We just caught up."

"So I was a *shooter* a long time ago. So what? That doesn't make me a murderer today!"

Di Bacco jumped to his feet and put his face an inch away from mine.

"No, but it makes you a scumbag in any year. You shoot porn. Maybe it's not hardcore anymore, but I've been looking over your recent work and it's still just as sick. You're a twisted, drug-addicted pimp, pervert, and killer, and you're going down for that girl's murder!"

I stood up and said, "I didn't kill anyone, and I've never been convicted of anything. I'm clean. I don't have anything to do with pornography. I'm a fashion photographer. My work appears in the best magazines in the country, and when my attorneys get through with you and your bootlicking stormtroopers, you'll be lucky to get gigs as meter maids!"

Di Bacco turned purple with indignant rage and punched me in the face, knocking me backward into, and then out of, my chair. One of the silent detectives grabbed Di Bacco and held him back. The other detective stood over me to make sure I didn't try anything. I wasn't about to make a move on this guy. He punched like he had a steam iron in his hand. I wasn't going to see how his kicking skills matched up by giving him an excuse to treat me like a soccer ball.

I wiped my mouth and looked up at Di Bacco. My teeth

felt loose and tasted salty from the blood, but I managed to speak. "Do you really think I'm so stupid that I'd kill some-one and then leave the body in my front yard? Are you such an idiot that you can't smell a setup when it's poking you in the face?"

"That's exactly what you wanted us to believe. Everyone knew you were with her. If she just disappeared or turned up dead in an alley you would be the obvious suspect. This way the case was so simple that it made it look like a setup. You think you're a smart guy, Bracken, but that reverse-psychology shit went out with the hula hoop."

The clerk entered the room again and approached Di Bacco. He whispered into Di Bacco's ear, then exited the room.

Di Bacco calmed down a bit and pulled away from the detective who was restraining him, straightening his suit and tie.

"Your shysters are here," he said glumly. Then he spoke to the detective standing over me. "Get him up and proper."

The detective helped me to my feet and put me back in the chair.

The clerk entered the room again, this time accompanied by Martin Smith and Bob Tate, my attorneys-at-large.

"It's about time," I said. I had called them over four hours earlier and was beginning to lose hope that they were going to show.

The attorneys looked at the blood around my mouth and then at Di Bacco, whose hair was mussed from the activity, and immediately sized up the situation.

"Doing a little fifties-style interrogating, Lieutenant?" Martin Smith asked, ignoring my comment.

Di Bacco said nothing. The clerk handed him a folded piece of paper.

"What's that, Lieutenant?" Bob Tate asked.

"Wouldn't be a writ from the DA releasing our client and his vehicle by any chance, would it?" Martin Smith piped in.

"You know damn well what it is," Di Bacco said. He was pissed. The system was about to fuck him again. Smith and Tate had spent their four hours productively.

Bob Tate looked down at me and smiled. "Seems these guys got a little carried away, Nick. Their paperwork didn't stick. We got the coke bust tossed out. So someone left a body near your premises? That doesn't give these gentlemen the right to search your house for drugs. That was one weak warrant, Lieutenant."

"Your *client* is still a murder suspect," Di Bacco said.

"Are you ready to charge him?" Smith asked.

"Think carefully, Lieutenant. You only have one shot at it," Tate added. They were in rhythm now, each coming in on the last word of the other's sentence, trying to tag-team Di Bacco into frustrated submission.

"Is your case strong enough?"

"Paperwork up to date?"

"You don't want another O. J. on your hands, do you?"

"Heads rolled on that one."

"The DA isn't so sure that Nick makes such a perfect suspect. He doesn't feel that the case is . . . what was the word he used?"

"Airtight."

"Right. He thinks caution is not your strongest personality trait."

"I'd say our client's condition would attest to that. I hope there's not going to be an ugly police brutality suit in this."

"You mean to go with the false arrest case we already have brewing?"

"Precisely."

"Book rights on this alone will be worth a fortune."

"To say nothing of the TV movie deal."

Martin Smith looked at Bob Tate as if he had suddenly been engulfed in a fiery epiphany. "Hey . . . We're going to be rich!"

Di Bacco was seething.

I couldn't control my smile. I loved watching these guys work. They were having a lot of fun at Di Bacco's expense.

"What's it going to be, Lieutenant?" Tate asked.

Di Bacco crumpled the note and stared down at me.

"You're free to leave the station," Di Bacco said. "But like they say in the movies, don't leave town. It might look suspicious."

I stood up and smiled at Di Bacco.

"Got no reason to go anywhere. I'm innocent."

3

Tate and Smith led me out of the interrogation room, down the hall to freedom. We passed the crowded bullpen. Cops were everywhere, filing paperwork, questioning suspects and witnesses, gabbing on the phones.

Detective Thompson sat with Patti, the redhead that Candice was hanging with at the party, and a black-leather-jacketed tough guy with three days of growth on his face.

Patti looked over and spotted me. "That's him," she said in her Texas drawl. "That's the guy Candy introduced me to last night!"

"Are you sure?" Thompson asked.

"Believe me, mister, I know that's the guy. . . . Nick Gardner—that's the name he gave me. That's the guy! He killed Candice!" She got to her feet and made like she was going to run at me. Thompson grabbed her and held her fast.

I started to move toward them. Smith and Tate took me by either arm and pulled me away, toward Processing.

"Recognize him, Angelo?" Thompson asked the guy in the leather jacket.

"Never seen him before," Angelo said, looking me straight in the eye from across the room. "Never gonna forget him, either."

I didn't like the sound of that.

PART VII

Looking *innocent can be just as important as* being *innocent.*
—Bob Tate

1

Tate and Smith got me through Processing in record time and with a minimum of fuss. They gave me a lecture during the ride to the impound to pick up my car. I had retained them three years earlier to handle my legal for the company that Lou and I started, but I had chosen them not only because Smith had a great rep at contract law but also because Tate was considered one of the finer criminal defense attorneys in southern California. I had a secret agenda in wanting to develop a relationship with these guys and now it was all starting to come out. I had hoped I would never have to play these cards, but I wanted to be ready if the time ever came. Obviously the time was now.

"Nick, we're very disappointed in you," Tate said. Smith was driving, Tate was in the front passenger seat of the Mercedes looking over the headrest at me in the back. This kind of trouble was more Tate's specialty, so he had the ball and he was running with it. "Why didn't you play straight with us? We consider it a breach of trust when one of our clients presents himself as somebody he is not."

"I never did that. My name *is* Nick Gardner."

"Only because you had it changed in 1990. The question is *why?*"

"I don't think you want to know the whole story. It may compromise your position while representing me."

"We are seriously considering *not* representing you."

"Why is that?"

"I told you. We don't like getting into things we don't understand. If you can't be truthful with us, then we can't effectively defend you. We have no idea what other skeletons are going to come rattling out of the closet if we have to go to trial."

"I didn't kill that girl. I'm innocent."

"Sometimes that is not as important as you may think."

"What do you mean?"

"If a jury gets involved, *they* will decide whether you are guilty or innocent based on law and/or intuition. If there is a gray area in the law, intuition will win. *Looking* innocent can be just as important as *being* innocent. If you have a shady past that the prosecutors can bring into play, believe me, they will."

Martin Smith suddenly spoke up. "What's the deal with the porn busts, Nick?"

I swallowed hard. I was going to have to deal with this. It was time to come clean with someone. It might as well be a couple of lawyers. Considering the moral compromises these guys made every day, they were the last people who should be passing judgment on me.

"They were simple pandering charges. Since the cops have trouble making porn charges stick with the First Amendment and all, they would try to nail us on prostitution and pimping, claiming that sex for hire wasn't protected by the Constitution, even though the actors were performing on film. I got a suspended sentence the first time, but I did five months in County on the second charge."

"How did you get wrapped up in porn in the first place?" Tate asked.

"It's what I used to do for a living a long time ago." I said. "It was how I learned to be a photographer. I worked my way up through the porn world as an assistant, then a still photographer, then a shooter."

"What's a shooter?" Tate asked.

"It's slang for cameraman. Any cameraman might call himself a shooter, but the guys who shoot loops were always referred to that way. If you wanted to make a quick loop and didn't know anything about camera, you hired a shooter."

"What's a loop?" Smith asked.

"Short little porn flicks that were popular back in the sixties and seventies. They'd run anywhere from five to twenty minutes long. They used them in the jerk-off booths and sold them to guys who had Super 8 projectors at home. This was all before video hit. I hear the loop business really took a dive after that. Porn went legit once the country could rent the stuff at the local mom-and-pop video store on the corner. It wasn't just for dirty old men anymore. But I got out just as all that was starting to happen."

"How did you 'get out'?" Smith asked.

"I went to Europe and started over in fashion. I worked my way up, learned my craft, and got good at it. You'd be surprised how many of the same techniques used in porn are used in fashion photography. It was easier than you would think."

"Why Europe?" Tate asked. I was being cross-examined by my own attorneys. Tate could sense the deeper problems inherent in my story and he was determined to get to the bottom of it all.

"I had some trouble on one of my shoots here," I confessed. I couldn't say more even though I knew it was going to have to come out.

"C'mon, give," Tate pressed. He was close and he knew it.

"A girl died."

Smith slammed on the brakes and pulled the car over to the side of the road. He turned and stared at me over his seat. His eyes looked crazy. Tate appeared perfectly calm, as if he had guessed the nature of the confession much earlier.

"Goddamn, Nick," Smith squawked, "what the hell did you do?"

"I didn't do anything," I protested. "I was just shooting a loop for a guy, and he and a guy who was working for him got carried away and accidentally killed a girl during the shoot. I didn't have anything to do with it. I was behind the camera the whole time. I freaked out and took off. I had to get out of there. I didn't want to go to jail again and I didn't want to get killed by the two guys who did it, so I split. I jumped a red-eye to London, then skipped to France. I lived in a little town on the outskirts of Paris for a few months and watched the *L.A. Times* for news of the girl's death. When none ever appeared I figured the guys must have disposed of her somehow. She was just another runaway. I don't even think anybody was looking for her."

"You were an accomplice to a capital crime, Nick," Smith said. He was pale. He'd defended his share of scum in his day, but this seemed to be getting to him.

"I'm telling you I didn't do anything."

"Why didn't you go to the police?" Tate asked coolly.

"For the same reason I didn't want to have to tell you guys about this. I figured I'd get the same reaction. If my attorneys think I'm guilty and immoral after hearing five minutes of the story, how do you think the police would have reacted?"

"Good point," Tate said, not disagreeing with my opinion of their opinions.

"I was young and I was scared. I had been in France the year before doing work for a soft-core guy and I liked the place. I thought I could disappear until whatever was going to happen blew over."

"And nothing ever happened."

"Exactly. But I no longer had the stomach for that kind of work. I was too freaked out. I took a job as a camera assistant for a fashion photographer. The money was shit, but I didn't need much. I learned a lot from the old guy and when he died I took over some of his client list."

"You didn't kill him too, did you Nick?" Martin Smith asked half jokingly. I just sat and stared at him. I was getting sick of his nonsense. This wasn't funny to me. It was my life.

"Ease up, Marty," Tate said. "I think Nick deserves the same benefit of the doubt that you give your oil clients during tax time."

Smith thought about it for a moment and some of the disgust drained from his face. "I'm sorry, Nick," he said, "I don't know what came over me. I'm reacting to this thing like some faggot juror that we would dismiss in about five seconds."

"It's understandable," I said. "It's how I would feel if I didn't know the whole story. If I hadn't lived the fucking thing myself. I don't expect anyone to believe me. That's why I changed my name and tried to turn my back on the past. But it looks like it's finally catching up with me."

"It doesn't have to," Tate said. "The two cases don't have

anything to do with each other. Not legally. As far as we know, the first case isn't a case at all. It doesn't even exist. If you are square with us and offer full disclosure we will make sure it cannot be played if we end up in court on the Candice Bishop case."

"You're still willing to represent me?"

Tate glanced at Smith for a brief second before answering. He wanted to make sure his partner wasn't going to throw up.

"Of course," Tate said. "We're attorneys. It's what we do."

With that Smith put the car in gear and pulled back onto the road. No more words were spoken for the duration of the ride.

2

It was a little after eight in the morning when I got back to my house. The ordeal had taken all night and I was exhausted. I was pleased to see that no reporters were haunting my place. Tate and Smith had managed to keep the details of my release confidential and the fires were keeping the scavengers busy elsewhere. As far as the media people were concerned, I was still cooling my heels in county lockup. They'd be pissed when they realized I had slipped out beneath their very noses.

Once inside the house I saw that the answering machine was blinking frantically, but I was too tired to deal with it. The phone rang as I passed it and the machine picked up. My voice droned out of the speaker; I don't lay music, poems, jokes, or gags on my messages as is the norm for most L.A. answering machines, just a simple "I'm not here. Leave a message." Short and sweet. Well, at least short. After the tone I heard Lou screaming on the machine.

"Nick! Motherfucker! Pick up this goddamn phone! I know you're there! Pick it up!"

It sounded like he was about to have a heart attack. I picked up the receiver.

"What is it, Lou?"

"What is it?" He continued shouting, as if it was going to make a difference. "It's the end of the fucking world is what it is. You seen the *Times*?"

"No."

"You're the star of the day. You managed to knock Michael Jackson and Mike Tyson down to the bottom of the front page. Happy?"

"What do you think?"

"I think you better get your ass over here and tell me what the fuck is going on. We got to figure out what we're gonna do."

I considered arguing with him, or even hanging up on him, but then thought better of it. The sun was already getting hot and I could tell I wasn't going to get to sleep. I was too wired. I was so tired that I was beyond sleep as a solution.

"I'll be in the office in forty-five minutes," I said.

"See you there." Lou hung up.

I put the phone down in its cradle and it rang immediately. I picked it up, thinking it was Lou calling back with something he forgot. A deep voice crackled on the line.

"Nick Bracken?"

I was shocked, totally caught off guard. I tried to keep my composure, fearing a trap of some sort.

"Who's calling, please?" I asked, as if I was a manservant.

"Nick, it's your father. This is Greg Bracken." The voice was tremulous, as if spoken from a deathbed. It was a voice I had not heard in fifteen years.

"There's no one by that name here," I responded. I was about to hang up the phone, but I found that my hands were shaking as severely as the voice on the other end of the line.

"Please don't hang up, Nick," the voice pleaded. "It's been a long time. So very long."

"What do you want?" I asked. My voice had become almost a whisper.

"I just wanted to know it was you. I saw the paper this morning and I thought it was you but I couldn't believe it. I thought you were dead long ago."

"As far as you were concerned, I was."

"But why?"

"I don't want to get into it."

"Nick, you owe me an explanation." The voice seemed to be strengthening with resolve.

"I don't owe you anything. You owed *us*. Your wife and your kid. You made your choice. She died, you know. Two years after you left."

"I know." The voice was weak again.

"They said it was pneumonia, but let me tell you—it was grief. She never got over you. You trashed her life."

"I went crazy. It was a midlife crisis. I thought I was in love with that girl."

"I always wondered, how'd that work out?" I asked sarcastically, my voice now strengthening with a resolve of its own.

"We lived in Kansas City for five years. She left me for a city maintenance worker."

"Tough break," I said without sympathy.

"I tried to find you when I came back, but you had disappeared."

"You were too late, old man. You're too late now."

"I want to see you."

"Forget it. If I see you I'll step on your neck."

There was silence on the other end of the line.

"Where are you?" I asked.

"La Jolla. I'm in a nursing home. My lungs . . ."

"The wages of sin, huh?"

"Nick, this business about you in the paper, is there any truth to it?"

"It's all true," I said, trying to inflict as much cruelty on him as possible. "You taught me well."

"Perhaps it's best that Elizabeth didn't live to see this."

With that I managed to hang up the phone. It began ringing again before I could reach the door. I left it to collect with all the other messages that I would be ignoring later on the answering machine.

3

I was sitting on the couch in Lou's office when he got there. A small green-shaded desk lamp partially illuminated the room. A plaque bearing the name Wide-Eyed Productions decorated the wall above my head. The name for the company had been Lou's idea. He liked to consider himself an idea man and that had been one of them. It was his major contribution to the company, other than the seed cash he had kicked in to get us started. He was a good negotiator. I had been cutting good deals before we partnered up and I could have continued on my own, but there was something comforting in not having to do that, not having to deal with the weaseling of the clients and the bullshit when it came time to collect. Lou had earned his share of the partnership, as hard as it was for me to admit. And I had been left alone to do the work. To make my magic. To bust my ass so the fat cats in the ad agencies could get rich pawning my silly-ass chromes to their clients for ten times what they paid me. The more I thought about it, the more I missed the porn world. There was an honesty inherent in the grit of it all that was absent from the "real" world. The "legit" world. In the porn world you were paid an honest dollar for an honest day's work. It was usually cash and it was paid on the spot. No bullshit. No chasing deadbeats for your wages. No suits throwing their lame ideas at you.

I handed Lou a glass of whiskey that I had prepoured for him. I was already half through a glass myself. He sipped the whiskey. His hands shook a little as he drank. He was taking this even harder than I was. He seemed to be sensing that his meal ticket might be imploding.

Lou took a seat behind his large marble desk. He refilled his glass from a bottle of AA Kentucky bourbon he kept next to the phone when no one was around. He threw down a newspaper on the desk in front of me. The headline read:

FASHION PHOTOGRAPHER LINKED TO PORNO QUEEN MURDER

Lou picked up the paper and shook it for emphasis.

" 'Fashion Photographer Linked to Porno Queen Murder.' If we're going to get headlines like this from the *Times*, think what the *Enquirer* is going to do to us."

I rubbed my forehead with both hands. I was lost.

"C'mon, Lou. I'm in trouble."

"Tell me about it. We've had four cancellations since I spoke with you this morning, and it's *Sunday*. I can't wait to see what tomorrow brings. I've been on the phone with John Casablanca trying to convince him that you won't carve up his models if he sends them to work with us. If this keeps up we'll be lucky to book the cover of *Soldier of Fortune*."

"It's not funny," I said.

"I'm not laughing. Want to tell me what happened?" He seemed to be calming down.

"Nothing . . . I mean . . . I met this girl at a party Friday night. She was hot, but she was crazy too."

"Nothing new in that."

"No. But there was something different about this one. She was nuts all right, but she seemed to have a brain. It was just fucked up. She was real schizo. I don't know, maybe it was the dope. Fuck, I knew that chick was trouble."

"Then why didn't you back off?"

"If you had seen her you'd understand."

"I can see her right here in the paper. Everyone can. The girl was a hooker and a porn actress. I thought you were smarter than this. Can't you spot a pro anymore?"

I picked up the paper to look at the story.

"She was a porn actress?"

"It's all right there in black and fucking white. She did porn. And she had been arrested for prostitution twice. Two times."

It was there all right. The woman's name was Candice Bishop, just as I had been told. I hadn't remembered hearing her last name the night I met her and it didn't really seem relevant at the time. Candice had performed in more than forty hard-core porn flicks under a wide variety of names, usually Candice King or Kandy Kane or some variation on the Candice/Candy theme. Aliases were common practice in the porn industry for a variety of reasons. She had dropped out of the business last year due to unspecified "health reasons." The writer of the article speculated that the demand for tapes starring Candice Bishop was about to soar. Nothing like actually dying to jump-start a dead career. The public has a definite taste for necrophilia. Even the porno-loving public.

The article went on to say that Candice had been picked up on the street for pandering once back in 1987, then she did a brief stint in Sybil Brand Correctional Institute for her second arrest in '88. She was busted while working for a high-class escort service. The vice squad nailed her and twelve other girls with a sting operation the papers had dubbed "Sweet Charity's Baker's Dozen Bust," Charity being the name of the woman running the escort service. The cops had gotten a lot of bad press on the whole thing. Seems the taxpayers weren't so happy with the fact that so much of their hard-earned cash was being spent on a bunch of cops trying to get a pack of cute hookers in bed and on videotape. This was before Heidi Fleiss became a national treasure. Anyway, Candice's time in the slam must have clued her that she needed a better way to work, so she went into porn and became an immediate star. I had never heard of her or seen her, but then again I had not had anything to do with the porn world in over a decade. I was way before her time.

I was mentioned none too complimentarily throughout the article as the man last seen with Candice Bishop, quite possibly the man who had killed her, although they did not come right out and say that, due to the slim chance that they could face a libel suit. They managed to imply plenty anyway. Speculation ranged from my hiring her for her services to some kind of bizarre Svengali theory that actually proposed I may have been behind her entire career as a porno star and hooker. When these newspaper guys got hold of something they managed to make pornographers look like Sunday school teachers. There was no firm ground I could sue them on. They danced around the hard facts with words like "alleged" and "suspected" and they quoted a variety of unnamed sources to take the heat of any malicious intent that could be read into the editorial tone of the piece, which was, however, supposed to be a news article. It was going to be another trial by media and this time I was going to be the victim.

I threw the paper down on the desk in disgust.

"It looks bad," I admitted.

"No shit," Lou said. "I think you should take some time off."

I was starting to get a clearer picture of Lou's attitude. I was quickly becoming a liability. He wanted to save the ship before it sank, even if *I* was supposed to be the captain. I got the distinct feeling that I was getting eased out of my own company.

"What are you saying, Lou?"

"Just that we need a low profile right now."

"Are you going to be behind me on this or not?"

"To tell you the truth, partner, I'd like to be so far behind you that I'm invisible."

I got up and dropped my glass onto Lou's desk, sloshing booze all over the newspaper.

"Thanks, buddy," I said as I walked out. "I'll be in touch."

My wife thinks I'm not being loyal enough to Nick. She thinks I should stand by him, you know, like Kardashian and O.J. or something. But I say bullshit on that. Not only is it bad for business, but frankly, if you kill someone the way they say Nick killed that girl, I don't want you in my life. You're persona non grata around here. Sure, Nick was my pal. We made a lot of dough together. We partied together. He had helped me out of rough times, but fuck, you have to draw the line somewhere.

—Lou Collins

PART VIII

Nobody makes anyone do anything.
—Jennifer Joyner

1

I cruised along Santa Monica Boulevard in the Lamborghini. I didn't know what to do, but I didn't want to go home. I needed someone to talk to. Someone who might believe me. I headed over to West L.A., to Jennifer Joyner's condo. She had a one bedroom on the border between West L.A. and Beverly Hills. Two blocks over and she would have had to pay an extra thirty grand for the place.

I banged on Jennifer's door. No response. I banged again. Finally the door opened and Jennifer peered over the chain-lock. She was disheveled, almost plain looking without the trappings, messy on top of it, still half asleep, or so she seemed.

"What the fuck are you doing here?" Jennifer asked. "I thought you were in jail."

"Sorry to disappoint you."

"What do you want?"

"I need to talk to you."

"Do you know what time it is? Get out of here."

She started to shut the door. I jammed my foot into the crack.

"Please let me in."

"If you don't leave I'll call the police."

"What's your problem?"

"*My* problem? It's ten-thirty in the morning and I've got a killer stuck in my doorway! That's my problem."

"Do you really believe I killed that girl?"

Jennifer stared silently at me for a long time. Too long. I turned and started to walk quickly down the hall. Jennifer shut her door and I could hear the chain being dropped. She opened the door and stepped out into the hall.

"Nick."

I stopped, turned, and faced her.

"This is dumb of me, but come on in," she said.

Jennifer ushered me into her place and poured me a cup of coffee. We sat at the breakfast table, morning light softly illuminating the room. She seemed nervous, which was understandable, but she said nothing, as if she was afraid of what she might hear if she asked me what she wanted to ask. I tried to relieve her silent curiosity.

"I have no idea what happened to that girl, Jenn. I passed out around three-thirty or four. She must've gotten a ride out of there with someone else."

"Then why was she found in your Dumpster?"

"Maybe her boyfriend did it and put her there out of spite . . . or maybe she never left at all. Maybe she ran into someone on PCH."

"One of your neighbors?" Her eyes were suddenly bright. She *wanted* to believe me.

"Maybe," I replied. "Or someone visiting one of my neighbors. Or someone just driving by. I don't know. It's all so crazy. If only I knew more about her, it might make some sense. How well did *you* know her?"

"I didn't. I never saw her before Mark's party."

I thought about that for a moment.

"Mark Pecchia's the key to all this," I said.

Something flickered behind Jennifer's eyes. I couldn't read it, but I had sparked something in her memory. There *was* a connection.

"He knows all about her," I continued. "He could tell me something that would help."

"I don't think you'd be very welcome at Mark's house right now," she said. "I mean, everyone thinks you killed a girl that he introduced you to. The cops were all over him yesterday. He bitched me out on the phone until midnight last night."

"You could talk to him for me."

"I don't want to get involved in this."

"You're already involved. You made me go to that party."

"Nobody makes anyone do anything."

She was right, but beyond that, she wanted none of the blame and it was obvious that she was feeling some.

"I'm innocent, Jennifer," I said quietly and sincerely.

She looked deep into my eyes, trying to figure out whether she should believe me or not.

"Maybe," she said softly.

"That's a start," I said.

———

I could believe a lot of things about Nick, but not that he was a killer. If you told me he fucked someone to death, maybe. But chop them up? Not Nick. That kind of behavior would require something Nick just doesn't have in his personal makeup—commitment.

—Jennifer Joyner

———

It was afternoon before I had the stomach to return to my house. A small cluster of paparazzi had gathered under my carport, awaiting my arrival. I hit the remote and scattered them like roaches as I pulled into the garage. I hit the remote again and almost crushed a number of them with the closing garage door. Fuck 'em.

The interior of my house was still a wreck. The cops had taken anything that vaguely hinted of evidence. I closed all the blinds to defend my privacy from an oceanside assault by the paparazzi.

I went upstairs and sat in a lounge chair on my second-story deck, away from the prying eyes of the media. I just sat there, staring out at the ocean. I still hadn't slept. My eyes were red, my hair frazzled. My five o'clock shadow was at twelve o'clock. I ran the last forty-eight hours through my head over and over, trying to make some sense out of all that had happened. None of it had any central thread of logic. It appeared that a series of seemingly random events had conspired to totally fuck up my life. But I knew it wasn't random. There was some form in the mist, but I couldn't make it out.

I could hear a commotion coming from the house to my right, the north side of my house. Even over the waves rolling onto shore, the distinct sound of my neighbor yelling at his wife was loud and clear.

Teddy Vincent is an actor. Or at least he used to be. A golden-haired surfer from Huntington Beach who made a series of successful "family" films as a kid in the late seventies and early eighties; the nineties hadn't been so good to him. He had shown great promise of breaking the mold of failed child actor in a couple of adult roles in mid-eighties action films, but a mixture of rude behavior and drug abuse had put him on bad terms with the studios. He was now relegated to low-budget schlock and straight-to-video erotic thrillers, the kind of crap that made the high-quality porn films of the late seventies look like modern classics.

Teddy had three problems, really. His ego, his wife, and co-caine. Teddy was insanely jealous of his wife, Maria. At the same time, his ego demanded constant gratification from a series of new-to-the-business bimbos. As is the case with most philanderers, he liked to accuse Maria of the same acts of infidelity that he was perpetrating. When cocaine came into play, things could get violent. I had called the police on Teddy two times in the last year for beating his wife. Maria refused to press charges on either occasion, despite her bat-tered and bruised face.

Teddy stepped out onto his deck, still yelling at his wife. He wrapped things up with "Shut the fuck up, cunt!" and took a drag off a glass pipe that presumably held cocaine. Teddy was a smoker. He had a lot in common with Candice Bishop. They both enjoyed the crack rush and it had similarly dis-rupted both of their respective careers, even if Teddy's career had been in what would have been considered "legit" movies by comparison to Candice's oeuvre.

Teddy let the narcotic wave flow through him and stood motionless, looking out over the ocean. After a few minutes he turned and saw that I was sitting on my deck.

"Hey, Gardner, how's it hanging, asshole?"

Needless to say, our relationship had gone downhill a bit after my calls to the police. I wasn't going to respond to him, but I wasn't going to give him the satisfaction of looking away either. I just stared at him, hoping he would go back into his house.

"So I see you finally got a taste of the cops yourself, huh?" he continued. "I may have hit my wife, but I never chopped her up."

"Give it time," I said, unable to stay quiet any longer.

"Fuck you, jailtail."

Maria was suddenly out on the deck.

"Get in here, Teddy, and leave Nick alone," she pleaded with him. She was high also.

"You still gonna defend that asshole, even after what he's done?" Teddy asked her.

"I don't know what he's done and neither do you."

"He killed that girl fifteen feet from our bedroom window, you stupid bitch. Don't you get it?"

"Whatever. Just get inside. You're making a fool of yourself."

Maria tugged at his arm and he pulled away violently, raising his hand as if he was going to slap her.

"Get the fuck off me, woman. I'll smack the shit out of you. Think he'll call the cops this time? No fucking way."

She shrank back, then reached out for him again. He slapped her in the face and she turned away from him and looked at the ground. She stood frozen there, waiting to see what would happen next.

Teddy looked over at me and smiled a rather boyish smile. "How about it, Gardner? Want to call the cops?" he goaded.

I stood up and walked over to the rail. His balcony was only six feet away from mine. I could jump it if I had to.

"Tell you what, crackhead," I said as ominously as I could. "You touch her again and I'll be stuffing another Dumpster."

Threatening a guy like Teddy Vincent was not my style, but I thought my newfound notoriety might save Maria Vincent some bruises, or worse.

Teddy looked at me as if he was seeing a monster. The drugs were twisting him up inside and whatever effect my words were having on him was being magnified through a coke-flavored haze. His eyes got wide and he looked genuinely scared.

A helicopter bearing photographers buzzed overhead, startling all of us. The paparazzi weren't going to let me off the hook that easily. They had technology on their side.

Maria pulled on Teddy's arm again and said, "Let's go in, honey." The slap seemed to be long forgotten.

Teddy looked up at the helicopter, then over at me. "You're a sick fuck, Gardner. I hope you fucking rot in jail."

Teddy and Maria disappeared into their house and the chopper came lower to get a better look at me. I flipped them off and went inside.

The action had finally supplied me with enough adrenaline to give me the strength and interest to shower and shave. I thought it would make me feel better. It did—for about five minutes. Then the bottom fell out. I lay down in bed. I was beat, but I couldn't get to sleep. I stared at the fish tank for about an hour before I passed out.

My exhaustion was so great that I never managed to find a truly deep and peaceful sleep. I dreamed with the kind of lucid imagery that is usually the product of drugs or alcohol. The dreams were so vivid that I couldn't relax properly. I'm not clear on the content, but the whole experience was so jangling that I might as well have stayed awake. As sleep goes, it was a bust.

3

After a few hours of tossing and turning I awoke to the smell of smoke. The Santa Anas were blowing in from Thousand Oaks again. I walked out onto my deck and looked for the smoke. The sounds of helicopters echoed from every direction, but this time they weren't looking for me. They were working the blaze. The media folks were out in force, capturing every tragic second of other people's misery. Oh well, at least I wouldn't be on page one again in the morning. I hoped.

There was a moon out and it had turned blood red from the smoke in the air. My house was in no immediate danger. Living by the beach was more of a high-tide risk in the Boo. The mountain dwellers had to deal with the fires and the mud slides. We got the storms and the tidal waves.

I went back in and lay down. I still wasn't feeling very good. The fish seemed agitated, darting erratically around the tank, as if they could sense the potential threat of the fire in the air.

Then the fire made me remember something. The lighter in Candice Bishop's purse; the words *The Eight Ball* inscribed on the side. It was probably a restaurant or club that she frequented. Maybe someone there would know more about her.

I got out of bed fast. Too fast. The room started spinning big time. I held still for a few seconds and regained my composure. I dialed 411 and asked for the number of The Eight Ball. They didn't have a listing so I tried San Fernando Valley Information. The 818 operator had the number and I dialed it immediately. I had a sneaking suspicion what kind of place this would be and I was right. It was a strip club deep in the Valley. I struggled to get dressed. It was almost midnight. I'd have to move quickly if I was going to get to The Eight Ball before it closed.

I backed the Lamborghini out of my garage and stopped. The paparazzi were gone, off to the fires I supposed, but my next-door neighbor, Robert Momberg, had just pulled up and was getting out of his Range Rover. It was funny how many people in show business had Range Rovers, Land Cruisers, and Jeeps. Most of them never braved rougher terrain than the Paramount backlot. It was as if they were preparing for Armageddon. Some kind of hip Judgment Day when they would have to load up and get the hell out of town fast like packs of hardened survivalists. It was all part of the tough-guy image.

Robert lived in the house immediately to the south of me; Teddy Vincent was one door north of me. I was wedged between these two slices of ham like bread in an inverted deli sandwich.

Robert Momberg came over to talk. He had a handsome face, fit for the daytime soap opera in which he starred, but it was late and he looked frazzled. I was now clean shaven and feeling fresh. My hair was slicked back into place. My day was just starting, Robert's was winding down.

"Hey, Nick," Robert mumbled. His voice sounded rough, like he'd been up all night drinking hot whiskey.

"What's up, Robert? You look beat."

"Late nights at the studio this week. We're stockpiling shows in case the director's strike happens next month. . . . Heard about the trouble. Everything okay?"

"It's all just a big mistake. We're working it out."

"That's good. It's a bitch about the fires, huh?"

"Yeah."

"I heard forty homes have burned."

"That's bad."

We stared at each other for a minute, not really knowing what to say. Neither of us really gave a shit if forty homes had burned, as long as none of them was ours, but we had to at least *appear* civilized. Robert seemed to have something else on his mind.

"Where you headed now?" he asked.

"Business," I said.

We looked at each other suspiciously, each of us wondering what the other was doing the morning Candice Bishop was killed. It was almost comic.

"Well, I better get some sleep," Robert said. "Gotta be up at four."

"See you."

"Yeah. I might have a barbecue next weekend. Drop in."

"Thanks."

Robert partied hard on the weekends. Starlets of all shapes and sizes flowed through his doorway. Occasionally I got a little of the overflow, but I doubted that this invitation was sincere in light of recent events. His was an uncomfortable politeness born of kissing up to craven characters on a daily basis.

Robert turned and walked toward his house. I let his "Gotta be up at four" sentence sink in a little, then I backed out onto PCH and hauled ass toward the city.

4

I cruised over the 405 freeway into the Valley and got off on Victory Boulevard. I hung a left on Van Nuys Boulevard and went north, entering an industrial-park zone. An unlikely location for a strip joint, but it hadn't slowed any of the fans down. I made a left on Raymer Street and immediately saw the large neon sign flashing The Eight Ball. By the time I pulled into the crowded parking lot of The Eight Ball it was almost one o'clock in the morning. I got lucky. This was one of the full-nude clubs in the San Fernando Valley that didn't close until 4 A.M. They couldn't serve alcohol due to the raw nature of the entertainment, so juice or sodas or near beer would have to do if you were thirsty, but this freed them from the two o'clock curfew that a "real" bar would have to obey.

The place even had valets. I decided to park the Lamborghini myself and gave the guy a five for allowing it. I found a vacant spot way in the back of the lot. The place was jamming. I walked through the parking lot looking at the vehicles owned by the denizens of The Eight Ball. BMWs and Jaguars competed for space with Jeeps, muscle cars, toughed-out motorcycles, and rusty pickup trucks.

I went through the bronze double doorway into The Eight Ball. The place was dark, packed, loud, and happening. Neon trimmed the walls. Topless and bottomless dancers occupied three separate dance floors like a Ringling Brothers for horny guys. Rock music blasted the girls into wild gyrations as a wide spectrum of men dropped cash on the mirrored floors near their feet or whatever else happened to be there at the time. There were at least two different bachelor parties scattered among the spectators. Men on their worst behavior coming to see women the way they thought God intended them—naked, flailing, and bent over.

The dancers were stylish and quite acrobatic. Floor-to-ceiling-length bronze poles were placed strategically on the stages and the girls had no trouble shimmying up and down them upside down and every which way they could; whatever it took to turn up the heat. One of the dancers' favorite moves entailed climbing all the way up the pole to the ceiling, doing a backbend until they were upside down, and then quickly sliding back to earth that way, stopping an inch away from a concussion. Once arriving back on the ground the dancers usually did a slow cartwheel over until they were right side up and could go into a full split all in one smooth, fluid motion. Men ejaculated dollar bills onto the dance floor whenever they were particularly pleased, which was often.

"Table dances" were also available for twenty bucks a song. You pick the girl and she takes you to a semiprivate booth to do a little dance for you, sans clothing. She strips, bends right over, and backs up into your face, eye to eye so to speak. It's a great way to satisfy curiosity without any complications. You can sample the wares for less than dinner would cost on a regular date and see more than the average woman would probably show you even with the lights off. All within five minutes of meeting your dream girl. Touching was not allowed. Of course there are benefits to such restrictions. No disease. No discussion. No drugs. A spending cap. And, of course, no jail time. There was even a glass booth where you could help your favorite dancer take a shower, in full view of the establishment's bouncers and all the other clientele, of course, but a loofa is a loofa. If you wanted full contact you could have a lap dance, but the girls had to remain fully clothed for that action and you were not allowed to touch them. They could touch you, however, and if you didn't mind a dry hump it could be worth the twenty bucks a song. Some guys would strap a condom on under their clothes, wait for the two-songs-for-one special and try to take it all the way to get full value for their dollar.

I went to the bar and ordered an orange juice, then I

turned and watched the dancers work the crowd. The girls
were high quality for this sort of place, better looking than
most of these sorry-assed guys would ever get to see naked
in real life. It was an honest establishment. Strictly run and
well organized. Everybody wins at The Eight Ball.

I sat watching the spectacle for a while and began to wonder what I thought I was going to find at this place. What had
I come for? I stopped a passing barmaid dressed in skimpy
nothings.

"What's your name, honey?" I asked.

The girl touched a small plastic name tag over her left
breast.

"Maxine. Can't you read?"

"It's dark in here."

"Your eyes will adjust," Maxine said. Then she took my
hand and rubbed my fingers along the raised letters on the
tag. I could feel her chest pulsate under the plastic.

"Say it with me. . . ." She spelled out her name: "M-A-X-
I-N-E . . ."

I joined in and said her name with her as she repeated it.
"Maxine," we said together.

"That better, 'honey'?" she asked, gently mocking my chau-
vinistic familiarity.

"Yeah."

"So what can I do for you? You want a table dance?"

"Maybe later. Actually, I was wondering if you had seen a
girl around here?"

"What do you think you just touched? String cheese?"

"I'm looking for someone specific, a girl named Candice
Bishop. . . . Sometimes she went by the name Candice King
or Kandy Kane."

"Candy? She doesn't work here anymore. Hasn't for a few months now."

I let this register. Candice had worked here. Maxine must have been in a cave for the last few days. She appeared to have no knowledge of Candice's death.

"When did she quit?" I asked.

"Didn't quit. Jorge fired her."

"What happened?"

"I don't know. You'd have to ask Jorge."

"Is Jorge around?"

"He's in his office. What's so special about Candy? Won't I do? I'm pretty good in a pinch."

"I bet you are."

"Hey, you're not a cop are you?"

"No," I said. "Could you show me to Jorge's office?"

"Customers aren't allowed in there . . . but I can go get him for you."

"You're great."

She took my hand and rubbed it across the name tag again. "Remember, M-A-X-I-N-E."

"I'm not about to forget."

Maxine moved off to get Jorge.

I turned my attention back to the stages. Dancers were trading places on the center stage. The new dancer was Candice's friend, Patti Weigel, the redhead from the party. Another piece of the puzzle dropped into place, but I still couldn't see the frame.

I watched Patti shimmy and shake across the floor, occasionally dropping one side or the other of her bikini top to expose some tit to the crowd. She had some good moves. Very sexy. She did one entire song before she lost the top completely at the beginning of a Janis Joplin tune. She was a little underdeveloped for this line of work, but what she had was real, unlike most of the other dancers. She began working on the bottom of the string bikini to make up for her shortcomings. She teased the crowd with glimpses of her bush by pulling the fabric from side to side, even sliding it up between the crack, parting the Red Sea. She was a natural redhead. Either that or she had purchased *two* bottles of the same dye. Patti turned her back to where I was sitting, then she bent forward and slid her bikini bottom all the way to the floor and smiled at me, both vertically and horizontally. She looked at me from between her legs and we made eye contact. I was a good twenty feet away from her and the place was dark outside of the stage lights on the dancers, but she managed to recognize me nevertheless, even though her head was upside down at the time. A look of shock washed over her face.

Patti straightened up and continued dancing, but she was having a hard time of it. She kept looking over at me, trying to make sure I was really who she thought I was. Her concentration was completely blown. Finally she rushed off the stage before her song was over, leaving the thirty-odd dollars that had hit the floor in praise of her talents resting right where they lay. The crowd grumbled. There was some kind of chaos going on backstage because the next dancer was not yet ready to come out. She finally made her appearance. She had blond hair and huge breasts. The crowd was happy again.

I was getting nervous. I considered splitting while the splitting was good. I finished my OJ and stood up from the bar. A diminutive, dignified-looking Spanish man in his fifties was suddenly at my side. He was Jorge Alonzo, owner of The Eight Ball.

"What's the problem?" Jorge asked.

"No problem," I replied. "I'm looking for a girl who used

to work here. I met her last year when I was in from New York. Her name is Candice Bishop."

"She's no longer with us."

"That's what I heard. . . . What happened?"

I could see Patti coming out from behind the dressing room curtain in the distance, wrapping a robe around her naked body. The guy in the black leather jacket that Detective Thompson called "Angelo" at the police station soon joined her. She pointed over at me and Angelo started through the crowded room with Patti hot on his heels. I knew I had only a few moments to find out whatever I was going to find out. There was about to be major trouble.

"Candice had an accident," Jorge continued.

"What kind of accident?"

"Candice passed away two days ago."

Angelo and Patti were suddenly beside Jorge.

"He should know, Jorge," Angelo said. "This is the piece of shit that killed her!"

"What?" Jorge's face seemed to expand upon hearing this. Other men gathering around us reacted to the news as well. They were obviously friends of Angelo's or Candice's or both.

Patti looked at Jorge and said, "He's the one."

"I didn't kill any—"

Before I could finish my sentence Angelo delivered a serious roundhouse punch to my ear. I was knocked backwards against the bar. My arm caught the padded railing, saving me from hitting the floor. I straightened up and tried to shake the cobwebs from my head. My ears were ringing. Angelo threw another roundhouse. I blocked the punch and he tried again. I blocked again and wrapped my arm around Angelo's arm, lifting under his elbow, then I delivered a straight flat palm strike with my free hand to Angelo's jaw. Angelo stumbled back and fell into a table full of empty beer glasses. He hadn't expected any resistance.

"Take it out of here, boys," Jorge said coldly.

Three burly fuckers grabbed me and shoved me toward the rear exit. Two of them were dressed like Angelo, full-on bikers; the third guy looked like he had just stepped out of a hunting magazine. Plaid wool shirt, overalls, hunting boots, the works. He was ready to bag some game. Angelo got to his feet and followed us. Patti stayed with Jorge. She was smiling with satisfaction.

I could see the cocktail waitress, Maxine, standing off to the side, watching it all. She rushed over to a pay phone and dropped a quarter. I was hoping she was calling 911 and not more guys to come over and help beat on me.

I was shoved out the back door of The Eight Ball onto the asphalt of the parking lot. The three guys stood aside and let Angelo approach me. Angelo rubbed his jaw.

"That karate shit ain't gonna do you no good in this parkin' lot," he said.

I got to my feet. My clothes had been ruined. My face wasn't doing so good either. The right side was starting to swell where it had been hit. Angelo seemed to have more respect for my prowess than he needed. I had picked up a little savate when I lived in France, but I was no karate expert. Far from it. I was just winging the business, trying to make it look good. Bar fights had never been my forte.

Angelo moved closer. I kicked his leg hard to keep up the illusion of competence. I got lucky and nailed him right on the crown of his kneecap. Anyone else's knee might have shattered. Angelo just did a little spin and hit the pavement.

I leaned up against an old car, a late-sixties Plymouth Road-runner. Angelo got to his feet. He favored the leg as he approached me again.

"I don't want any more trouble," I said.

"I know you don't," Angelo replied. He rushed forward, head down like a tackle, and smashed into my gut, slamming me against the car. He hit me low again and brought his head up into my chin. The back of my head cracked on the roof of the Plymouth.

I pressed back against the car, bleeding, out of breath. Angelo was just getting started. He straightened up in front of me and removed a pair of spiked brass knuckles from his pocket. He slipped them on his right hand and rubbed them lovingly. One punch from that shit and I'd be drinking through a straw for the next three months.

"Candy was my girl. . . . I loved her!" Angelo shouted.

He threw the punch and I dropped to the ground. Angelo's fist shattered the car window above my head, cutting his hand and slicing his arm in the process.

"Motherfucker!" Angelo yelled. He grabbed the bottom of his arm trying to slow the bleeding. I put a size-eleven shoe directly into his balls, heel first. He lifted into the air, the wind, among other things, exiting his body. Angelo crumpled on the ground when he landed.

The three other guys rushed forward and began kicking the living shit out of me. I was pinned on the ground against the car, with nowhere to go. I tried to crawl under the car, but the hunter grabbed my leg and pulled me back out. He socked me in the jaw for my brazen attempt to survive.

Two police cars suddenly roared into the parking lot on either side of us, lights spinning, sirens wailing. Lately I hadn't liked looking at the cops. Now I was overjoyed. Red and blue suddenly became my favorite colors.

Four cops jumped out of the cars. Two carried shotguns. This place must have had a reputation because these guys came ready to rumble. One of the cops fired a shotgun blast into the air and yelled, "Break it up!"

The boys ceased stomping me and immediately put their hands on top of their heads. They knew the routine. I laid my head down on the asphalt and took a little nap.

5

I sat in the corner of a crowded jail cell in Van Nuys watching my fellow prisoners. They were the dregs of society, gangbangers, drunks, and felons, but they all looked better than I did at the moment. My clothes had been literally ripped to shreds, dried blood caked my face, bruises covered 80 percent of my body. My bottom lip was split and my head was throbbing. Nobody fucked with me. There seemed to be an air of sympathy for me in the cell, I was so pathetic looking. Or maybe they just figured that there wasn't much left to pick over.

Lieutenant Archibald Di Bacco stepped in front of the cell and yelled, "Gardner!"

I looked over at Di Bacco, but I didn't move.

"I came down as soon as I heard they had you over here," Di Bacco said. "Liked our tank so much you decided to try the Valley branch?"

"Want something?" I asked.

"I was just wondering what you thought you were doing? I know about the old 'returning to the scene of the crime' bit, but I thought you'd wait awhile. That wasn't very smart."

He was piecing together a story far more credible than mine actually was.

"I've never been in that place before tonight, Di Bacco. My story hasn't changed."

"That's just what it is, too, mister. A story! You probably met the girl there in the first place and you were going back to find fresh meat! You just can't get enough. You're certifiable."

I got up and walked through the crowd toward Di Bacco. My cellmates were enjoying the dog and pony show. I was hoping to flash enough of the tough-guy act to keep everyone off me when bedtime rolled around.

"I went there to do *your* job," I said. "Because I know if I leave it up to you and your lackeys I'll end up in jail."

"Newsflash: You *are* in jail."

This brought sporadic laughter from my fellow inmates. One of the guys yelled "Fuck you" at Di Bacco. Not everyone enjoys sarcasm.

A clerk approached the holding tank.

"Not for long," I said to Di Bacco. I was developing a sixth sense for freedom.

The clerk called into the cell, "Nick Gardner?"

"Right here," I said.

"Your attorneys are here," the clerk said.

I smiled at Di Bacco as the clerk unlocked and opened the cell door. The clerk escorted me toward the exit. Di Bacco followed behind. We passed two of the guys that slammed me in the parking lot in another tank, then Angelo and the hunter among other prisoners in a third cell. The cops had separated us for our own good.

I stopped and looked in at Angelo.

"I didn't do it, man," I said. I don't know why I wanted him to know I was innocent, but I did. I wanted him to believe it. Not just so that he'd leave me alone, but for my own peace of mind. I wanted to convince *someone,* even if it was the guy who just helped kick the shit out of me. I wanted someone to believe me, so I could continue believing it myself.

Angelo moved closer to the bars. He wasn't buying it. "See you on the outside, dude," he said in his best Clint Eastwood. Wild, wild west all the way.

Di Bacco moved me forward with two fingers in my back. "He won't be out that long," Di Bacco told Angelo.

6

I sat with Martin Smith and Bob Tate in a sterile white conference room in the back of the Van Nuys Police Department. I could tell that neither of them was in a very good mood. I was becoming a burden to the firm. The cops had provided three hard chairs and a small white table to write on in case anyone needed to make out a suicide note.

"Nick," Martin Smith began, "you're not making things any easier on us playing detective."

"Yeah," Bob Tate chirped in. "Let's cut the Mike Wallace shit, okay, buddy?"

"If I don't find out what really happened that night, no one will," I said.

"That's fine by us," Smith said.

"The less you do, the better," Tate added. They were getting into their rhythm now, each stepping on the last word of the other's sentence. When used against the cops I thought it was funny. Now it was simply annoying.

"Right now the police don't have a solid case."

"But they're working on it."

"You keep stirring things up and they may get enough on you to press charges."

"Maybe even get a conviction."

I looked at them both sternly. "You guys think I'm guilty."

"We didn't say that," Smith said.

"Neither of us said that," Tate added.

"It's not our job to determine whether you're guilty or innocent."

"We just want to make sure you don't do any time."

I stood up and paced nervously.

"This is great: Even my attorneys don't believe me."

"We believe you, Nick."

"Yes. . . . If that's what you want, we believe you."

I slammed my fist down on the table.

"Listen to me goddamnit! I'm innocent. I was set up! I don't know how or why but the whole thing was a fucking setup!"

Martin Smith got up and touched me on the shoulder.

"Ease up, Nick. We had a long talk about this. We're with you on this."

"We're on your side."

"We just want you to be a little more . . ."

"Prudent."

"We don't want to go to trial on this thing."

"And if we go to trial we don't want to . . ."

"Lose."

"So do us a favor. Just stay home. Get some rest."

"Catch up on your reading."

"Do whatever you want. But stay away from anything related to this case."

"Things are bad enough already."

"Please promise not to do any more detective work."

I stood up straight and looked at them both. I realized I was totally on my own. A look of calm resolve washed over me. I decided to lie to them.

"Whatever you guys say."

PART IX

Sounds like you're in deep shit.
—Paul Cutshaw

1

Tate and Smith arranged for my bail and dropped me off in the parking lot of The Eight Ball to get my car. At least it hadn't been impounded this time. Once again the sun was coming up as I tasted freedom. I took the 101 out to Topanga Canyon and drove over the mountains to avoid the rush-hour traffic heading into town over the 405. A dark canopy of smoke hung over Topanga like a rain tarp at a barbecue. The smoke was so thick that it was creating twilight conditions. I had to turn on my headlights to get over the pass.

I turned on the tube when I got home and caught the early news. The fires that were consuming Laguna and Thousand Oaks and parts of Malibu were also consuming the better part of the local news coverage, knocking my story down to a brief twenty-second mention leading into a commercial break. After the O. J. debacle, my tale of murder and sleaze was barely worth covering. The ante had been upped in ways that were still not fully comprehendible.

The news guys were really making a meal out of the fires.

They had already created fancy logos and coined phrases like *Firestorm!* and *Malibu Inferno.* They were reducing the latest disaster to just another miniseries. Natural disasters always made for good TV. They have it all: tragedy, spectacle, heroism, greed, love, lost pets, the works. And the production values are footed by the population. The cost to the networks is minimal. It's much cheaper to shoot fires ravaging Tom Selleck's house than to hire Tom Selleck to be in a movie, yet they get to legally exploit his name. It was fabulous. I hoped the fires would keep burning for a year, but I knew they'd put them out in a few days and then the media dogs would get hungry and turn on me again.

I read the *Times;* they had managed to pick up on my arrest the night before, but the story was buried all the way back on page six. There were minor rumblings that the trouble might somehow be tied to the Candice Bishop murder, but once again the legal department went out of its way to make sure the paper was *legally* absent malice. They really knew how to walk that razor blade.

I turned off the phone and turned the volume down on the answering machine so I could crash. I slept for six or seven hours, waking around three in the afternoon. I staggered around the house for about an hour, wandering aimlessly, not knowing what to do next. I played my messages back on the answering machine. I had twenty or so calls of support from various people who wanted to kiss my ass and gain employment in the future (if there was one) and there were six different calls that basically consisted of death threats. My number was unlisted so I had to assume these calls were made by people who knew me or knew other people who knew me. A handful of reporters had discovered the number and were requesting interviews. They each promised to tell *my* side of the story. I also received a call from Lou which fell somewhere between support and a death threat. He suggested that it would be a good idea if I took some time off to "gather my thoughts." That roughly translated to "Get away from me, you scare me, I'm afraid I'm going to go broke just for knowing you."

I checked the news for the latest updates on the fires. Instead I got the latest update on my life. The TV guys were starting to focus more attention on my case. They had dug up some facts about my past and had put together a collage of some of my old porn work and some of my more recent print ads, drawing juvenile conclusions about the artist and his roots. There were also interviews with Candice Bishop's friends and relatives back in her hometown of Scranton, Pennsylvania. Reaction ranged from absolute shock to total revulsion to apathetic acceptance. Candice had always been a wild one, an ex-boyfriend said. She was always so sweet, a girl from high school remarked tearfully. We knew it was just a matter of time, her father, a rough-looking son of a bitch, said. He seemed to be weeping no tears for his long-lost daughter. They weren't even going to have the body returned home.

"Let her rest where she wanted to live," Daddy said.

None of the family would be attending the services, which were going to be held at Forest Lawn on Saturday, the day after the coroner planned to release the body. Members of the adult film community were springing for the tab.

The whole thing was so depressing I just crawled back into bed and went to sleep. I was out for the night.

I slept restlessly. I finally decided to get up early and catch the sunrise. I sat out on my deck and watched the water turn colors in the growing light. I deeply inhaled the fresh sea air and steeled myself for a trip into town. I took a very long, hot shower and felt my muscles relax for the first time in days. I still looked like a bruised eggplant. There would be no getting around that.

I drove over to the studio. Neither Lou nor our secretary, Iris, were in their offices. I went into my darkroom and sifted through prints and negatives, packing the ones I wanted into a large box. If I was going to go away, *anywhere,* I wanted my best work placed somewhere for safekeeping.

Whitney, my camera assistant, passed the doorway, saw me, came back, and stuck his head into the room.

"What's the haps, boss?" Whitney asked.

"I'm splitting for a while."

Whitney entered the darkroom. He was dressed in torn jeans and a fatigue shirt. He had an earring in the shape of a silver skull in his left earlobe. He wore his hair in long dreadlocks. He was a white guy, but he wanted desperately to be black. I continued working without looking at Whitney as he spoke.

"Yo, I mean what's happening with your face? Someone do a rain dance on it?" he asked.

"Something like that."

"Let's go get the fucker!"

"Forget it."

"Were you strapped?"

"You know I don't do that."

"Maybe you should. City's gettin' crazier."

"Not my style."

"Gotta tell you somethin', boss. Black an' blue ain't in this year either."

I finally looked up at Whitney. He had a point.

"You know what happened, right?" I asked.

"I read the paper. They say you killed Kandy King, but I think it's bullshit."

"Why's that?"

"Well, boss, I figure you for a lot of things, but that kind of action don't rock with the pattern, know what I mean? Sure, you *could* have done it, but you're too smart to let it go down the way it went."

"Thanks," I said. "I think."

"Ever see that babe's flicks?"

"No."

"I have. She had a hot box. Fuckin' shame someone did that to her. You gonna find the asshole?"

"I'm going to try."

"Figured. Let me know if you want a little firepower to go with the hound dogs."

"I will."

Whitney gave a nod and disappeared around the corner. I went back to work, but a lot of what he said stayed with me. My paranoia allowed even Whitney to enter the list of possible suspects, although he was as unlikely a candidate as one could imagine. Just another straw to be grabbed at out of desperation. The guy offers me help and I want to pin a murder on him. I was in a place in my head that I never knew existed. And I wanted away from it.

3

After finishing in the darkroom, I went into my office and started working the phones. I knew I only had so much time and I wanted to get to the bottom of the story while I still had my freedom. I wanted to find out everything I could about Candice Bishop, and to do that it was becoming painfully obvious that I would have to go back in time a little, back to a time when I walked in the world Candice had been working the last few years.

The pornography business is a small, tightly contained organism. It's a huge business, yielding over four billion dollars a year, but, aside from the fringe elements and amateurs, the community itself is comparatively microscopic. Everybody knows everybody else. For the most part, they all get along. They certainly get along a lot better than most of the people I've met in the more "legitimate" photo mediums. The media boys like to present porn manufacturers and distributors as sleaze mongers and back alley weasels. On average, nothing could be further from the truth. Most of them are family oriented. They are usually honest businessmen and women who treat their employees with respect and pay their bills on time. If they owe you money, you *will* get paid. I have not always found this to be the case in the legit world. I've been deadbeated by some of the richest men in show business. The bigger they are, the more they think they have the right to fuck you over.

Paul Cutshaw had been a friend of mine way back in the days when I was a shooter. He ran a company called Royal Publishing, printing high-quality adult magazines and creating jackets for other distributors' Super 8 films. He was a midrange success in the business. He had never been greedy about it. He just wanted enough money to keep food on the table for his family. Of course, the table *was* located in Beverly Hills.

I got Paul's current home number from Information. A housekeeper answered the phone when I called and informed me that Mr. Cutshaw was at his office in the Valley. She gave me the number. Unlike me, Paul Cutshaw was far from paranoid. He paid his taxes on time and never cheated on his wife. He was an upstanding member of the community and had nothing to fear from anyone. His life was an open book, even if more than a few pages of that book had naked people fornicating on them.

I dialed the number in the Valley and spoke with his secretary. Mr. Cutshaw was at lunch, but he had been gone quite a while and should be back any moment. I informed the young lady that I needed to see him today. I told her I was an old friend from many years ago and I was going to drive out and try to catch him when he got back. She asked me who she should say was coming.

"Tell him Nick Bracken is on his way," I said.

4

I took the Hollywood Freeway into the San Fernando Valley once again. Most people associate the porn industry with Los Angeles or New York, but the fact is 90 percent of the brain power behind the business is located in the San Fernando Valley. All the big guys bought warehouse land out there in the sixties and seventies when purchases like that were dirt cheap. They were dug in, entrenched in the war against the moral majority and the Internal Revenue Service. The feds had nailed a couple of the big fish in recent years. Unable to get pornography or pandering charges past the First Amendment, the government had fallen back on the IRS to produce results. Ever dependable, the taxmen succeeded in proving a number of big operators had not been reporting major income from the *peeps*—booths that customers would drop quarters into to watch short loops, the kind of stuff I used to shoot. They estimated millions had gone unreported, all in the form of quarters. It had been enough of a rap to put some of the biggest names in the business behind bars, including the infamous Rupert Herman who had eluded all forms of legal harassment for more than twenty-five years.

I had known Rupert well, back when I was a shooter. He was a great guy, one of the nicer men I'd ever done business with. He was always a gentleman. They didn't make guys like that anymore. The feds didn't give a damn. They dropped old Rupert into a minimum-security prison with all the other white-collar trash and he couldn't handle the confinement. One day he just up and walked away. It took them six months to catch up with him, but once they did he was screwed. He was currently serving out an extended sentence in Soledad, one of the worst maximum-security joints in California.

I cruised through an industrial area in North Hollywood. I recognized many of the buildings as establishments that I used to work for over a decade ago. They were all still there: World News, Concord Publishing, Paragon Entertainment, and the most famous of them all, Rupert Herman's Doc Jackson, makers of everything from the *Butterfly Tickler* to the *Black 18-Inch Double Dong*.

Paul Cutshaw's Royal Publishing was situated among these corporate giants. His company was small by comparison, but he still managed to fill two converted warehouses with magazines, offices, and employees.

I parked and studied the exterior of the buildings. When I knew Paul he had only one warehouse. Somewhere along the way he had expanded and purchased the sister building. A glass-enclosed walkway connected the two structures. They were gray brick, totally unassuming. They could have been packaging dried flowers in there for all anyone could tell. There were no guards, no watchdogs. No signs warning off trespassers. It was just a simple little business that dealt in fuck books.

I entered the main warehouse and walked along giant shelves stacked high with pallets of magazine cartons. Warehouse men worked through the building, but none of them paid me any heed.

Paul Cutshaw saw me through the glass window of his office and immediately came out and approached me, his hand outstretched, a big smile on his face. We met in the middle of the warehouse and shook hands warmly. Cutshaw looked like he hadn't aged a day in the last twelve years. He was a tall guy, a little on the geeky side. He had bright blue eyes and an expansive smile that made you want to like him and, more important, trust him. He was a great salesman because he believed every word he ever said. They were usually all true.

"Nick Bracken . . . son of a bitch . . . I never thought I'd see you again. What the hell happened to you?"

"I got out of the business a long time ago."

"No, I mean your face. What happened to your face?"

"Car accident."

"Not been your week, has it?"

"That's for sure."

We turned and walked toward Paul's office.

"Nasty business about you and Candy," he said.

"It's a frame job."

"What happened?" He seemed to be accepting the possibility that I was innocent, but I couldn't read him for sure. He seemed to be reserving judgment until the facts were in. He would have made a good juror.

"I spent the night with the girl," I said. "The next day they found her dead body and the murder weapon in my Dumpster. Someone set me up."

"Sounds like you're in deep shit."

"What did you know about this woman?"

"Only what I read in the magazines."

Paul reached into a box on a skid and pulled out a random magazine. He waved it in the air in front of me. It was a high-quality piece of slick color porn entitled *Sluts in Uniform.*

"*Sluts in Uniform* . . . Candy's in it."

He handed me the magazine and I flipped through it quickly. It was her all right. She was doing the same things in this magazine that she had done with me in the privacy of my home, only she was doing them with a wide variety of men and women, the lights were on, and people were taking pictures of the show.

We continued to walk down the aisle. Paul reached into sample boxes on each skid that we passed and handed me magazines. They all featured Candice Bishop, usually under the pseudonym Kandy Kane. Paul read off the titles as he handed them to me.

"*Aerobic Orgasms, Thrill Fuckers, Love Suckers, Blacks and Blondes, Pulp Friction, Backdoor Women, Load Warriors, Shaved Fun, Climax #2, Wet Blondes,* you name it, Candy was in it. She could have been as big as Seka. She was one of the busiest models in the business until about six months ago. We couldn't print 'em as fast as she was shooting them. We'll be coming out with fresh layouts of her for another couple of years."

"What happened six months ago? Why did she drop out?"

"She didn't drop out. She was forced out. Drugs caught up with her. What else? She had a coke problem for a long time, but when she finally got popular she went totally out of control. Nobody could work with her. She did a whole Marilyn Monroe trip, showing up hours late, when she showed up at all, blitzed out of her mind, throwing tantrums, extorting extra cash in the middle of shoots. None of my guys would use her. She ended up scabbing with a few of the fringe shooters for a little while, then she dropped out of sight about five or six months ago. I don't know what happened to her after that. Until a few days ago, of course."

I let the comment pass. I was sure there was no accusation intended. Not from a guy like Paul Cutshaw. He may not have known what happened to Candice when she left the porn business, but I knew. She had ended up titty-dancing at The Eight Ball for dollar bills until they couldn't take any more of her shenanigans either, but there was no point in sharing that information with Paul.

"Who were the last guys to work with her?" I asked.

"Funny, I just got a call this morning from Nate Boritzer offering me a still package that he's touting as 'Candy's Last Session.' He said the shots are only a month old, but I'd bet they're older. I had heard she was doing a lot of S-and-M stuff with him after she dropped out of the mainstream, but the market was so saturated with her image he couldn't move the chromes. I got the feeling he was just trying to peddle leftovers, but it'll be worth a look. Candy's going to be hot again for the next few months."

"Yeah."

We entered Paul's office. It was large and plush. Leather furniture, warm colors, family photos everywhere. There was no sign of porn in this inner sanctum.

"Drink?" Paul offered.

"No thanks," I said. I'd had enough to drink for a while.

"Have a seat."

I sat down on a soft burgundy sofa. Paul sat behind a large oak desk. He reminded me of Lou a little. The *business* was what he liked. He barely noticed what he was selling. He was just a big, goofy guy, happy to be alive and making money. A family man, working to put his kids through college.

"What's the story on this Nate guy?" I asked.

"Real lowlife. I tried to put him to work when he first hit town a few years ago . . . didn't work out. Booze, dope, messing with the models, he broke all the rules. A first-class burnout. I let him go after three months. He went freelance. His stuff's okay, sometimes. I buy something occasionally."

"Where can I find him?"

"He's got an old warehouse down in Venice. My secretary can give you the address. But I don't know what you're going to find out from him."

"I don't either. But I've got to start somewhere."

"He's a real space case," Paul said. "You'll be lucky if he even talks to you."

I looked around the room at all the family photos. Forty years of history stared back at me. Paul had well documented his life. He loved his family and he loved his friends and they were all up there on the wall to see.

"You still with Gloria?" I asked, wanting to get off the subject of the murder.

"Nineteen years next month. Johnny turned sixteen two

weeks ago, Sarah will be twelve in March. But you never met Sarah, did you?"

"No."

"They're great kids. They're the greatest. What about you? Ever settle down and get married?"

"Not yet."

"No kids?"

" 'Fraid not."

"What are you waiting for?"

"I don't think I'm cut out for the domestic life."

"That's what it's all about, you know, Nick? All this other stuff, the buildings, the businesses, movies, TV, sports, they're just distractions from the important things. Civilization has confused us as to what our real purpose is. Family, Nick. You gotta have family. They get you through the rough times."

"I just haven't met the right person yet."

"It'll happen for you. She's out there."

I changed the subject again. I was even more uncomfortable talking about family than I was talking about pornography and murder. I noticed a picture of Paul with one of his ex-partners from long ago.

"Whatever happened to Elliot Silver?" I asked.

"He died in '89. Colon cancer."

"That's too bad."

"Yeah. I miss him, but it seemed like some kind of perverse justice the way he went."

"How's that?"

"Everybody always used to tell me what an asshole Elliot was."

We both laughed. It was a short, nervous jolt of laughter that reminded me of the old days. Elliot *had* been a bit of an asshole. Paul was the class of the act, but Elliot did what had to be done. Deep down he was an okay guy. I could tell that Paul's affection for the man was sincere, despite his words. Paul's eyes showed a little more moisture when he stopped laughing than he would care to acknowledge. I decided not to continue about Elliot.

"Do you ever see David Rink anymore?" I asked.

Paul's expression darkened.

"No. I don't see David anymore. He's my main competition now, but I never see him. We had a falling out."

"David's still in the business?"

"David *is* the business nowadays. He's into it all, loops, features, videos, mags, he's even got a chain of stores going."

"Really?"

"Yeah. Maybe you should look him up. Candy did some work for him too."

"David knew Candice Bishop?"

"*Every*body knew Candy."

PART X

Look who's back from the dead.

—David Rink

1

I got Nate Boritzer's address from Paul's secretary and went down to meet the man. I wasn't ready to see David Rink again. Not yet. Maybe not ever. That was an encounter I was hoping to avoid altogether. We had unfinished business that I had no interest in finishing. I wanted to exhaust as many possibilities as I could before I got entangled in that mess.

Nate Boritzer was living in a small warehouse near the beach on the Venice boardwalk, just south of Santa Monica. The Santa Ana winds and the smoke from the fires had driven everyone in the city to the ocean. I had to pay ten bucks just for a parking space.

It didn't take long to find Nate Boritzer's building. He was in the heart of it all. He had quite a blatant location for a semi-pro pornographer. He probably went crazy looking at all that hot flesh strutting itself on the beach in front of his building. Then again, maybe he managed to do some recruiting from his perch by the ocean. I walked around the warehouse to see what I could see. I found a few filth-caked windows at ground

level that hadn't been boarded up or painted over. I rubbed
the dirt off one and looked inside.

The place was as different from the warehouses I had just
left as it could possibly be. It was ramshackle and almost
completely empty. Cobwebs were everywhere. Multicolored
paint remnants of various shoots splattered the floors. A man
I assumed to be Nate Boritzer was asleep on a cot in the middle of the main room. He looked unwashed, unkempt, and
unloved. Sunlight filtered through a skylight above and a few
broken windows around the circumference of the building.
A half-empty bottle of Bacardi 151 and about eighty cigarette
butts were on the floor around the cot. There was no other
furniture visible in the entire room. Nate's breathing was
heavy, punctuated by an occasional grinding snore.

I went to the front door and banged loudly. There was no
response. I rapped some more and finally I heard a voice yell,
"It's fucking *open!*"

I opened the door and entered. My footsteps echoed
throughout the hollow room as I approached Nate Boritzer.
Nate rolled over onto his face and curled up into a ball, not
wanting to deal with visitors. I stepped up to the foot of his
cot and stared down at him. He was deep in the clutches of
151-proof rum.

"Are you Nate Boritzer?"

Nate twisted his head around so that his left eye could look
up at me.

"Who wants to know?"

"My name is Nick Gardner. I'm here to ask you about a
model you used to work with, Candice Bishop."

"You a cop?"

"Just a friend."

Nate uncurled himself and tried to sit up. He stank of rum and cigarettes.

"Well, if you *are* a cop it looks like someone got into your ass pretty good."

"Plane crash," I said.

Nate tried to stand, then fell back onto the cot.

"Yeah. Me too," he said.

"When was the last time you saw Candice?"

"Who?"

"Candice Bishop. She also went by the names Candice King and Kandy Kane, among others."

"Never heard of her."

"That's funny. Paul Cutshaw said you called him this morning and offered him a layout featuring Candice."

"Paul who?"

This was going nowhere.

"I'd be very interested in seeing those chromes," I said. "I might even buy them from you."

"Too late. Sold 'em an hour ago."

"To who?"

"That's whom," Nate corrected me. There was something going on underneath his glazed expression. There was still a spark of intelligence lurking behind those bloodshot eyes.

"To *whom?*" I played along.

"A buyer."

Nate stood up and looked around the dilapidated warehouse. I was becoming totally bored and frustrated with his act.

"Uh listen, uh . . ." he muttered, trying to remember my name, or at least *acting* like he was trying to remember my name.

"Nick," I fed him, to get him to move on.

"Nick. Yeah. Uh, you think we could take this chat outside? I'm gettin' claustrophobic in here."

"Sure."

Nate picked up the bottle of 151, took a long slug, then offered it to me. I turned it down. Nate put his foot on the cot and gave it a good strong kick. The cot was on metal wheels. It rolled all the way across the empty floor and banged against the wall.

"Let's get out of here," he said. "The walls are closin' in."

We went out and walked along the boardwalk. We had no trouble blending in with the tapestry of weird that swirled around us. The Venice boardwalk offers a bigger collection of freaks, fairies, fantasies, and fuckups than Disneyland and Ripley's Believe It or Not all rolled into one. Nate and I belonged there.

Red clouds hung low over the ocean, both to the north and to the south of us. Smoke from the Malibu and Laguna fires was making its way into the ecosystem. Soon Santa Monica and Venice would be covered with soot and ash as well.

"Yeah, I knew Candy," Nate said, restarting the conversation somewhere in the middle. "She was a great piece. A real trooper. A total whore."

"When was the last time you saw her?"

"A few minutes ago. Didn't you see her skate by?"

"The girl is dead."

"The dead don't skate?" Nate asked.

"I'm wasting my time with you," I said.

"Time is relative, but life . . . life is a terminal illness. I think Nietzsche said that."

"I doubt it."

"Mmmm, maybe not."

"Can you at least tell me who bought that last session from you?"

"A friend."

"Who?"

"Guy named David. You don't know him."

"David Rink?"

Nate grunted. "Uh, well I guess you *do* know him."

That was what I was afraid of. Now I'd be forced to confront David Rink if I wanted to follow the trail of the pictures. It seemed inevitable from the start.

"When did you take those pictures?" I asked.

"What pictures?"

"You know what fucking pictures." My voice was starting to imply possible violence.

"Oh *those* pictures. Couple weeks ago."

We stopped at a chainlink fence and watched the weightlifters and aerobics freaks working out at Muscle Beach. I thought about strangling this jerk. I'm sure none of the jocks would have objected.

"Are you like this all the time?" I asked.

"Sometimes I get *really* fucked up."

That I would like to see. "Can you think of anybody who might have wanted to hurt Candice?" I continued.

Nate ignored the question. He was mesmerized, watching all the men and women pump themselves up in a desperate attempt to fight off age and death.

"You know what people are?" Nate asked. "Shit factories. If you took all the shit that a person produced by the time they're thirty you could fill ten Olympic-size swimming pools. Do you know how much shit that is?"

"About the same amount I've stepped through since I walked in your door," I said.

Nate didn't respond to that. He was on a roll and he wanted to finish his thoughts.

"Now multiply that amount by all those people over there. . . . Then by all those people down the sidewalk. . . . Think of the implications! We're talking about *oceans* and *oceans* of shit! Where does it all go?"

"The *ocean,* asshole," I said harshly.

I had had enough. I started to walk away. Nate looked out at the Pacific Ocean as if some great truth had just been revealed to him. A mystery had been solved.

"Hey! You're right!" he yelled. "I can see it, man! The ocean is full of shit! Holy Christ, I'm gonna have to sell my surfboard!" Nate laughed hysterically to himself. A couple of weightlifters suggested he stick his surfboard up his ass. He turned to them, dropped trou, and mooned them for their trouble.

"Do it *for* me, sailor," he squawked, then he stumbled back toward his warehouse, pants down around his ankles.

I picked up my pace out of there. I wanted to get as far away from the lunatic as quickly as possible. Even if it meant seeing my old friend David Rink.

2

I got on my car phone and called Paul Cutshaw. He gave me the name and address of David Rink's company, Fantasy City, Inc. It was out in Canoga Park, another bastion of the porn world deep in the San Fernando Valley. I called and asked to speak to Rink. The receptionist told me he was not available. I asked when he *would* be available. She asked me who I was. When I told her, she put me on hold. After a few minutes the

girl got back on the phone and said Mr. Rink could see me in
one hour. I said fine and headed out.

Traffic was light, so I was in Canoga Park in half an hour.
I grabbed a cup of coffee and a copy of the afternoon newspaper at Denny's to kill some time. The fires had been 95 percent contained. The weather had suddenly cooled, but the
Santa Anas were due to hit again in a day or so. Prepare for
the worst was the newspaper's advice. Wasn't it always?

My story and the story of Candice Bishop now occupied
three columns on page twenty. No new news. No good fuel
for the scandal fire. Instead I learned that a rising young
actor had died a little after 3 A.M. Sunday morning in the bathroom of a Hollywood nightclub called The Crisis Center.
Cause of death was rumored to be drug related. The Crisis
Center was owned by another hot young acting stud and the
two had been partying with a rogues' gallery of Junior Hollywood types in the club until the wee hours of the A.M. Sometime after closing someone mixed the wrong kind of drug
cocktail and the guy went into eight or nine minutes of con-
vulsions in the latrine before dying. The papers were already
prepping the kid to be this generation's James Dean. River
Phoenix was the more obvious comparison, but for some reason River's people had not managed to capitalize properly on
his demise. Dean was still the gold standard by which all
tragic young male death was measured. There was more
money to be made by the new dead guy's fixers if he was compared to Dean. Dean's people were annually taking in more
money forty years after his death than most actors make in a
lifetime of work. For some, dying is a good career move. You
could hear the memorabilia machinery starting up all over
town preparing to milk every dime possible out of the poor

guy's death. The story was tawdry and glitzy enough to make me feel a little easier about my situation. The names were much bigger surrounding this death than Candice Bishop's. This could be a smoke screen even denser than the one the fires had provided.

I finished my coffee, tossed the paper, and headed for a rendezvous with my past. David Rink and I went way back. To the very beginning of my career. We had been partners and the partnership had ended abruptly when I left the business. I had the feeling he felt betrayed in some way. David had never been the type to forgive and forget.

3

The outside of the Fantasy City, Inc., building was innocuous enough, a little fancier than Paul Cutshaw's place, but not by much. It appeared that it might be a good deal larger. The building seemed to go on a distance in the back, but the front was perfectly mundane. Just another business living out of a few connected warehouses in the Valley. The inside was a different matter altogether. It was a palace. There was an incredibly ornate waiting area immediately inside the entryway. Marble floors. High, triple-recessed ceilings. One entire wall of this room was made of rock with a waterfall cascading down the face into a large pool filled with big, healthy koi. Environmentally themed paintings lined the walls not made of water and rock. Antiques abounded. The furnishings in this room could easily be valued at over half a million dollars. Apparently no one cared that the moisture in the air would damage the rich wood grain of the furniture.

I looked around, impressed, then approached the recep-

tion desk. A young, perky, voluptuous girl was signing paperwork for a Federal Express agent who seemed quite
enamored with her. She completed the paperwork and he
completed his lame flirtations and skittered off. She looked
up at me and smiled a perfect smile.

"May I help you?" She spoke with the professionalism of
an airline stewardess.

"I'm here to see David Rink."

"And you are?"

"Nick. He's expecting me."

She picked up a phone.

"He's in editing. I'll ring him." She punched a few buttons.
"David? 'Nick' is here to see you. . . . Okay."

She hung up the phone and smiled. She stood up and
straightened the wrinkles from her beige shirtdress. She had
a great body. The outfit and the way she was wearing it reminded me of Candice Bishop. Then I realized: This girl was
probably a porn actress as well. She was working the "legit"
job as either a way in or a way out of the hardcore life.

"Come with me," she said. She turned and walked through
a set of gold double doors. I followed. She led me down a very
long, white hallway. More original art adorned the walls,
all by name artists. Doors along the hall led off to a dozen
offices and workrooms. I could see artists hunched over
drafting boards in some of the rooms, salesmen working the
phones in others. Young, energetic people bustled from office to office like ants respectfully obeying a higher order.

"What's your name?" I asked the receptionist.

"Nancy."

"You've got quite a place here, Nancy."

"We're moving soon. We've outgrown the space."

"Where are you going to go?"

"Probably out of the Valley. We've been looking at an estate in Beverly Hills that we're thinking about renovating."

"Sounds expensive."

"Gotta spend it to make it."

"That's what they say."

"Could I ask you a question? It's kind of personal."

"Fire away."

"What happened to your face?"

"Slipped in the shower."

"Ummmm."

She stopped in front of a door marked Editing Bay #5. "Here we are," she said as she threw the door open and ushered me in.

David Rink sat in front of an elaborate video editing console. A plump guy wearing funky-looking red glasses sat off to the side. He looked familiar, but I couldn't quite place him. They froze the image that they were working on so they wouldn't lose their place in the picture. On the multiple screens above the console I could see an attractive woman going down on some hundred-dollar-a-day stud from a variety of camera angles. The latest epic was being assembled for the masturbatory masses.

David Rink stood up and faced me.

"Look who's back from the dead," he said.

I extended my hand. David made no move to shake it. I dropped it to my side and tried not to let the brushback bother me.

"Hello, David. Been a long time."

"A couple of lifetimes, at least," he said.

———

Nick fucked me over big time. He got his ass in a sling
and then he cut and run. He didn't tell me shit about it,
other than a frantic phone call in the middle of the night
saying he was in trouble and had to skip town. He was
extremely sketchy with the details. He's a shit and a
coward. I can't believe we were ever friends.

—David Rink

———

David nodded at Nancy, releasing her. She looked at me
oddly and shrugged as she exited the room. I had no idea what
it meant.

David looked up at the frozen image on the main screen
of the editing console. The girl had a mouthful and was working it with precision. It was Nancy. Her hair was different, but
it was Nancy. The look and shrug now made sense. A casual
"whatever" apology to a man she had never met before. I understood. No matter how seasoned a professional became in
this business there were always moments of awkwardness.

"How do you like her?" David asked. "Cute, huh? Wonder
what her folks think?"

"I'm sure they're proud as hell," I said.

"Jesus Christ. What happened to your face?" It had taken
him long enough to notice.

"Got my ass kicked."

"That's terrible." He didn't sound particularly concerned
or sympathetic.

"I've felt better," I said flatly.

David suddenly seemed aware of the plump guy's presence, as if just realizing that he was in the room.

"Shit, I'm being rude. Nick, this is my associate, Morrie
Fein. Morrie, this is Nick Bracken . . . or should I say *Gard-
ner?* I hear that's what you've been calling yourself lately.
Which is it?"

There was more than a hint of bitterness and irony in the
way David spoke. I attempted to ignore the hostility. No time
for a pissing match with this guy. "Doesn't matter," I said.
"Nick will do."

Morrie stood up and shook my hand and then I recognized
him. He was the guy kissing Mark Pecchia's ass at the party;
the guy who had gotten us our drinks. I thought he worked
for Pecchia, but here he was, thick as thieves with David
Rink. What the hell was going on around here?

"Glad to meet you, Nick," Morrie fawned.

"Nick and I used to be partners, way back in the Dark
Ages," David told Morrie.

"Didn't I meet you at Mark Pecchia's house?" I asked Morrie.

"At the party?" Morrie asked.

"Yeah."

"Could be. I was pretty toasted that night. . . . I don't remember much."

"So, Nick," David said. "Let me show you around the place
and you can tell me what's on your mind."

"All right."

David led me toward the door. Morrie sat back down in
front of the fellatio-filled editing console.

"Nice meeting you, Nick," Morrie said.

"Again," I insisted.

"Again," he admitted.

Morrie Fein looked a little nervous.

PART XI

Sex rules the universe.

—David Rink

1

David Rink took me on a tour of the Fantasy City studio complex. It was a complete one-stop shop of pornography; sound stages, photo studios, processing labs, telemarketing offices, shipping warehouse, video duping rooms; the works. It was a country unto itself. David seemed quietly proud of the operation. I tried to act suitably impressed, but I really couldn't give a damn. I had left the business a long time ago and revisiting it was only stirring up bad memories. I had larger concerns on my mind. Life-and-death concerns. I explained the Candice Bishop situation to David in brief detail. Then I asked him what he knew about Candice.

"She worked for me plenty," David said. "But that was a long time ago."

"I thought you might be able to tell me some things about her personal life. Who were her friends? Who were her enemies?"

"Candice didn't have friends or enemies, only contacts," David said. "She was into money and drugs. If you couldn't supply her with either she wasn't interested in you. She did have this thing going with a guy named Angelo who liked to consider himself a manager, impresario, whatever. Sort of a Svengali of sleaze, if you know what I mean . . . a real pain in the ass. He used to strong-arm us into hiring him as a stud on her shoots—a two-for-one or none-at-all kind of proposition. He's a suckfish. A real jerk."

"Yeah. I've met the guy. Think *he* might have killed her?"

"How would I know? I'm not a cop." David was starting to lose what little patience he had with me. We entered a large, soundproofed stage. It was vacant at the time, but the amount of camera and lighting equipment scattered around the bedroom set indicated that they were getting heavy use out of the room. David gestured around the studio, as if I hadn't taken it all in properly yet.

"We have a complete complex here," David said. "I'm not just a shooter anymore. I handle every aspect of the business now. From production to marketing to distribution to retail sales." David gestured even more expansively, trying to give me a hint of his company's grandeur.

"I've got soundstages, a film lab, video duplicating house, ad agency, even my own printing presses for the mags and video boxes. I'm as close to a monopoly as you can get on the West Coast. I'm self-sufficient now. Completely self-sufficient."

"That's terrific, David. I'm glad you've done so well."

"Sure you are," he said sarcastically.

I could feel the tension coming off David like Santa Ana heat. I tried to move on.

"Where are you living now?" I asked.

"I'm back in my old loft."

"The loft we used to use as a studio?"

"Uh-huh. I had a house in Brentwood but I picked up a divorce last year and I gave the place to her."

"Sorry to hear that."

"I'd only known her a year. . . . It was impulsive."

He sounded genuinely hurt, not just by the fact that it hadn't worked out, but that he had been foolish enough to think that it would.

We went through a thick padded doorway, down another long hallway to a massive shipping warehouse that made Paul Cutshaw's place look infinitesimal by comparison. Racks and pallets of porn mags, films, and tapes were stacked to the thirty-foot-high ceilings.

"But why would you go back to the loft?" I asked. "You must be loaded."

"It's just temporary until I find a new place. I kept the loft after you split town so I could use it for downtown shoots. It's a nice location. I like the neighborhood."

"I hear a lot of artists have moved in around there."

"Yeah. It's become a very hip area. Can you believe it?"

A delivery man was unloading cases of video cassettes onto the warehouse dock from the back of a step van. He stopped and approached David.

"How you doin' today, Mr. Rink?" the man asked. He handed David an invoice on a clipboard.

"Great, Sal. And you?"

David checked the invoice against the number of boxes on the dock.

"Pretty good. My back's been acting up again."

"That's a bitch."

"Listen, we had to short you two cases of blank cassettes."

"Again?"

"I'll get 'em over to you first thing in the morning."

"Your company is slowing down my operation here."

"I'm real sorry. We just can't make 'em as fast as you need 'em. You guys are keeping us turnin' twenty-four hours a day."

"Guess we'll have to start manufacturing blank cassettes, too, eh, Nick?" David said to me as if we were still partners. He was having this guy on and strutting his stuff for me at the same time.

"Don't do that, Mr. Rink," Sal said. "We'd lose our best customer."

"Then tell Russell to get off his ass and fill our orders when we need them."

"You got it, Mr. R."

David signed the invoice and handed it to Sal. He noticed Sal eyeing the new porn magazines on the sample rack nearby.

"Want some reading material, Sal?"

Sal seemed a little embarrassed by the implications.

"My brother's in the hospital. It might cheer him up."

"Help yourself."

"Thanks, Mr. Rink."

Sal pulled the top copy from the invoice and handed it to David, then he began picking through the sample mags. David and I continued walking through the warehouse.

"That's the funny thing about this business, Nick," David said. "Everybody wants a look. Everybody is curious. Everybody takes if they can. Everybody is fascinated to see the fucking, but nobody wants to admit to the appeal. It's so hypocritical."

"I don't think the whole world revolves around porn," I said.

"You're naive."

"There are plenty of people who live without it."

"They may live without it, but only because they haven't stumbled across the right material yet. *Everyone* is turned on by something. Leave anyone alone in a room with the right magazine or video and they'll be grabbing themselves in less than five minutes. Anyone. I don't care if it's the pope. Then they'll be hooked. Sex rules the universe. Five billion customers can't be wrong."

"You don't think much of people, do you?" I asked.

"I *love* people. They're my business. Shit, they're my *product* . . . but you gotta face facts. Fucking's what it's all about. That's what makes the world go round. I just like to be up front about it."

"You've gotten awfully cynical in your old age."

"This used to be your bread and butter, too," David said. He was starting to get angry again. "When did *you* get religion?" he asked vehemently.

I laughed at myself and how ridiculous I must have sounded.

"Probably when they were reading me my rights," I answered.

David relaxed a little. An understanding smile creased his face.

"That'll do it," he said.

We walked in silence for a few moments and went through a doorway into a large room filled with printing presses. They were all working, every single one of them. Slick color pages rolled off the presses filled with consenting adults doing what consenting adults do. No kids, no animals, nothing kinky, nothing illegal, just pure clean fucking. David nodded and greeted his printers, a multiracial mix of old-timers and young trainees. They all seemed happy to see him.

"As you can tell, I'm very hands-on around here," David said over the clattering of the presses. "This is a big operation and I don't have much of a life outside of this building, but I like it. I've got a good crew. They're very loyal."

That was a direct hit. He was practically spitting on me and my lack of "loyalty" a decade ago. I knew we were closing in on a conflict. I decided to go for broke and try to get anything I could from him before I got tossed out on my ear.

"Nate Boritzer told me you bought the last photo session that Candice Bishop posed for."

"Just this morning. You must have found out before I did."

"Could I take a look at the chromes?"

David had heard enough. He snapped. "Look, what do you *really* want? What are you trying to get at?"

"Nothing," I said, a little startled at the bluntness of his attack. "I'm just trying to find some answers."

"What the hell kind of answers do you think you'll find in a bunch of porn chromes?"

"I don't know. Maybe some clue to her state of mind or who she was hanging around with. I'm totally in the dark, looking for whatever leads I can find."

"So you think *I'm* some kind of *lead* in your murder investigation?"

"Of course not. It's just that you bought the pictures."

"I buy pictures all the time. It's what I do for a living. What business is it of yours?"

I decided not to mention to David that I saw him at Mark Pecchia's party Friday night. Instead I tried to play on what little positive history I might have with him.

"Shit, David, I'm accused of *killing* that girl. Don't you want to help me?"

"Ten years ago you walked out on our partnership and broke all communication with me, now all of a sudden you show up asking for favors. You're unbelievable!"

"You know why it had to be the way it was."

"You didn't tell me shit. Just that you were in trouble and had to split."

"I couldn't give you details. I didn't want you dragged into the thing."

"So why the big change now?"

"I thought it had been long enough. I thought we could be civil about it all. I thought we could put it behind us."

"You didn't think too hard, did you?"

"I guess I was wrong."

"I guess you were."

I headed for the door. "See you," I said.

"Good-bye, Nick." There was a very bitter, very satisfied tone to David Rink's voice. He mumbled something to himself as I left, but it was drowned out by the gnashing and grinding sounds of the printing presses.

2

I went to a local bar to cool off. The encounter with David Rink had gone about the way I figured it would. Badly. I had learned nothing. I wasn't even sure what I was trying to discover. The pictures of Candice Bishop that Nate Boritzer had sold to David Rink could be of little consequence. They would just be more shots of her doing what she did best. I was using them as an excuse to revisit the past; something I had been working diligently to avoid for more than a decade. It was surprising how little had changed in that time. Sure, stars had risen and fallen, people had passed away, new people had entered the fray, technology had revolutionized certain aspects of the business, but the game was still basically being played the same.

The bottom line was that I hadn't gained any ground. I was no closer to extricating myself from this mess than when I first began snooping around. I had just gotten a few ass whippings for my trouble.

I kicked back two Tanqueray and tonics and felt a little better. I began to develop a renewed sense of confidence and a strange sensation of blind optimism. While I hadn't truly discovered anything specific in my travels, the alcohol convinced me that I might have accomplished some things nevertheless. I had stirred the pot. If anything was going to come up from the bottom, I had done my bit to loosen up the stew.

I left the bar and headed over the hill to my office. I was in the mood to have a conversation with Lou. When I got to the parking lot I saw that Lou's Bentley was in its spot. The master was in.

I entered Lou's outer office and approached Iris, our secretary. Iris was cute, in a plump sort of way, and about twenty years younger than Lou's long-suffering wife, Katie. Lou and Iris had been having an affair for the last six months, but neither of them would admit to it, even to me. I had respected the deception, not just in deference to Lou and Iris, but to Katie as well. Katie was a classy woman. I had spent much time with Lou and Katie when Lou and I first partnered up. Katie had earned my respect on many levels. I wouldn't feel right keeping a verified indiscretion from her. She was one of the few people I had met in L.A. who had a sense of honor.

I could not actively conspire against her, even for Lou and Iris.
Occasionally Lou would manage to sneak in a bit of model
action on top of it all, cheating on his wife and his mistress
simultaneously, but he never flaunted it and I did my best to
look the other way.

"Hi, Iris," I mumbled as I approached her desk.

"Your accountant has been calling you for two days," she
said. "He said there's going to be serious trouble if you don't
get some money into your accounts immediately."

"Trouble?" I said. "That's funny." I made a lot of money,
but I spent a lot as well. The wolves were always a few feet
away from the door, but now I had bigger wolves to worry
about. The kind of wolves that could put me in jail. I had trouble my accountant couldn't even comprehend. At the same
time, I needed to stay flush to keep my attorneys happy. Their
retainer had taken a big chunk out of my savings, but it was
only a drop in the bucket compared to what was ahead.

"Bob Tate called, too," Iris added. "Said it was important."

"Get him on the phone for me, please."

I went into my office and waited for Iris to buzz me. I
hadn't even gotten seated when the intercom blared.

"Bob Tate on line two," Iris said through the fuzzy speaker
system.

I picked up line two and sat behind my desk rigidly.

"What's up, Bob?" I asked with some trepidation.

"It's not looking good, Nick," he replied in a too-friendly
tone. "They're building a good case against you. I've got a
team of interns going over everything with fine-tooth combs,
but I wouldn't bank on any loopholes pulling us out of this
one. I want to ask you something, man to man, off the record,
but within the protection of our attorney/client privilege. . . ."

"I'm innocent, Bob," I said, anticipating the question. "I

did not do it. If I did, I would tell you right now. I mean it."

"You understand why I had to ask, don't you?"

"Yes."

"In a way it would be easier to defend you if you *were* guilty. At least we'd know what we were dealing with. We could work out an acceptable plea bargain. This kind of thing, you'd be out in about five years nowadays."

"Sorry I can't accommodate you. I didn't do it."

"You ever hear of Dale Holiday?"

"Who hasn't?"

"I want you to go see him. His office is in Brentwood. Can you be there at four?"

I checked my watch. It was almost three.

"Yeah. Give me the address."

I wrote it down on a piece of scrap paper.

"Nick, just tell Dale the whole story. Don't leave anything out. If he can't find out who did it, no one can."

Bob was trying to sound optimistic, but there was an underlying tone of desperation about it all.

"Thanks Bob," I said. "For everything."

"That's what we're here for. Stay out of trouble, okay, buddy?"

"I'll try."

I hung up and looked at the scrap of paper with Dale Holiday's name and address on it. If they were bringing this guy in on this I really *was* in trouble.

I headed for Lou's inner office.

"Nick, don't go in there yet," Iris said nervously. "He's on the phone—"

"Screw that noise."

I flung the door open and entered. Lou *was* on the phone. He looked up at me and showed me how irritated he was with a flick of his middle finger. I slammed the door shut behind me and smiled wickedly. I had caught him in the act.

"Gotta go, John," Lou said into the phone. "Don't forget, eight A.M., ten twenty-two Melrose. We're counting on you. . . . Right. See you tomorrow." Lou hung up the receiver.

"I hope you're making good money off *my* jobs," I said.

"If I could get you a gig, believe me, I would," Lou said. "I'm losing my shirt farming out our assignments."

"Then put me back to work."

"I could get more business for you if you had leprosy than I can right now. Between the girl and your little incident at the strip joint you're getting quite a reputation as a psycho. Plus I've had the cops on my ass every day since this started and I'm getting bored with the harassment."

"They can't do that."

"Well, they can and they are. That cop, Di Bacco, has it in for you in a bad way and it's eating into my racquetball game."

"So fucking sorry."

"Then do something about it."

"Like what? You think I *like* being in this mess? We're *partners*, man. I should be getting a little support from you."

"Partners, shmartners," Lou grumbled. "This business is about to go down the shitter and I'm not going to lose my ass 'cause you can't keep your dick in your pants."

"You're a fucker, Lou. A real fucker."

"Look, Nick, I'm sorry you're in this jam, but there's nothing I can do about it. I've got bills too. My life can't stop just because you're in a little trouble."

"A little trouble? I may be going to jail!"

My face was draining of color. I was sobering up fast and the truth was sinking in now. I wasn't going to get out of this mess. I was ruined and soon I wouldn't even have my freedom. I was in the middle of a terminal nightmare. Lou waved it all away with a simple gesture of his hand.

"You've got the best attorneys in town," he said. "They won't let you go to jail."

I sat down on his couch and stared at the floor. I felt the last bit of energy and courage float out of my body. I was beaten.

"They're about to run out of legal hocus-pocus," I said. "And when they do, I'm going down."

3

I arrived at Dale Holiday's office at a little after four. He was waiting for me. Dale Holiday is a small man with a ferret face and an equal talent for digging up shit. He is widely known as the "fixer to the stars," a private investigator who can place you in Hong Kong on the night you supposedly molested six young boys or sacrificed a goat on your neighbor's lawn. Holiday had been involved with "secret" investigations on some of the biggest Hollywood cases of the second half of the twentieth century. Most of his clients were still walking the streets as free citizens.

Dale Holiday was in his late fifties, but looked a good ten years younger. The amount of frantic energy that he put into his job seemed to be keeping him a few steps ahead of Father Time. He shook my hand with an enthusiasm that most people reserve for their first meeting with the pope or Elvis.

"Nice to meet you, Nick," he said excitedly. "Rough circumstances, I know, but what the hell? Marty and Bob have said a lot of nice things about you. Want coffee? A Coke?"

"No thanks."

"Have a seat."

I sat on a brown leather couch. The office was straight out of the forties. Redwood paneling and rich leather furnishings. The room had a claustrophobic, but luxuriant, feel about it and it smelled of fresh cedar, probably delivered via aerosol can.

"Tell me the story," Holiday said, sitting on the corner of his desk. "Give me everything, no matter how embarrassing or confidential or incriminating. I have a law degree and an affiliation with Marty and Bob, so we are protected by attorney/client privilege. Think of this room as your confessional. Everything you say here is protected by God and me."

He said "me" as if he was being generous to God by giving him first billing. Over the next twenty minutes I relayed the story to him in graphic detail. He had heard much of it from Smith and Tate, but I had details for him that the attorneys hadn't heard yet. I told him of my two neighbors on either side of my house, Robert Momberg, the soap actor who had been working late and getting up early as of late, and Teddy Vincent, the musclebound has-been who liked to freebase and beat women and was still harboring a grudge against me for having him busted on spousal abuse charges.

Holiday grew more and more excited as I gave him leads and suspects. He scribbled it all down furiously in a small reporter's notebook that he could carry in his breast pocket.

I told him about Candice's boyfriend, Angelo, and her girlfriend, Patti, from Texas. Then we discussed David Rink and Nate Boritzer, although their connection to any of this seemed tenuous at best, and I mentioned my suspicions about Mark Pecchia, although I wasn't exactly sure what I was suspicious about. They were all suspects as far as I was concerned. Even Jennifer Joyner. How could I be sure she wasn't some crazy stalker who freaked out and killed Candice out of some kind of jealous rage?

When I finished my bizarre burst of stream-of-consciousness paranoia Dale Holiday flipped his notebook over and laid it on the desk.

"I've got my work cut out for me," Holiday said with a ferret smile. "Actually it looks pretty simple."

I sat forward in amazement, my heart starting to race. Had this guy figured it out already? No wonder all the major talent agencies in town had him on retainer.

"Tell me," I said, hoping he could bring this nightmare to an end.

"Teddy Vincent," Holiday said. He didn't seem to see the need to elaborate.

"What makes you say that?"

"I've got a file on him that would choke Linda Lovelace. He's a bad boy. Sounds like a dream date for your girl."

I wondered if the porn reference was for my benefit or if it was just the way he talked, just a coincidence. I had the feeling he was trying to earn my confidence, show me he was one of the guys, an insider of the world I used to inhabit. There was something phony about this guy. He was another cheap actor in a town full of them. But maybe that was the problem. He'd been fixing for so much show biz trash that the act had worn off on him. No matter, he had honed in on the same similarities in appetites between Candice Bishop and Teddy Vincent that had struck me and now he wanted to make things happen. I had the feeling that Teddy was about to encounter some very rough road on his ever bumpy journey through life.

"If Vincent did it, I'll find out," Holiday continued. "Even if he didn't, he's a great guy to have as a neighbor considering the state of things."

I had never looked at it that way. Despite the optimism in Dale Holiday's voice, I felt a cloud of doom descending around me. All the shysters and shylocks in town weren't going to pull my fat out of the fire. I wasn't any legendary running back or movie star. I was an ex-pornographer with a shady past who had lived under an alias for the last decade. If a jury got hold of me, I'd be finished. If anything could be proven against Teddy Vincent or whoever the true murderer was, it would have to be ironclad in order to get me off the hook. Innuendo and slander against an easy target wouldn't do it. No, the only way I would walk away from this would be to get hard evidence against the killer or killers, and that sort of thing didn't look like it was going to drop out of the sky. Time was running out.

4

The sun was setting on the Pacific as I sped home. People were packing it in for the day. Empty picnic baskets and coolers were being loaded into cars; jet skis were being reeled onto their trailers; surfers were stripping off their wetsuits right alongside PCH and changing into civvies behind beach towels; homeless people were making their way to their favorite sleeping spots. All was normal except for the haze in the air that still hung low from all the recent fires. The Santa Ana winds were expected back soon. They would sweep the soot south, but they would also bring more heat and dryness, more risk of arson and wildfires.

I could see from a distance that the front of my house was thick with paparazzi. I had to time my approach appropriately. I hit the clicker for the garage door and came close to nailing a number of photographers as I turned into the driveway. My garage door opened barely in time as I came roaring in from PCH. I skidded to an abrupt halt inside the garage, an inch away from hitting the rear wall. The garage door closed automatically behind me and I sat staring at my face in the Lamborghini's rearview mirror. I felt calm for a moment, then I suddenly exploded with rage and frustration. I took it out on the steering wheel, slamming it with my fists, grabbing it, shaking it, trying to rip it right out of the dash. Fuck it. Fuck it all!

I entered the kitchen from the garage and turned on the lights in the house. I pulled my hair back off my face, composed myself, and walked through the house to the stairway that led up to my bedroom. I ignored the flashing light on the answering machine as I passed it on the stairwell. I no longer had any interest in anything anyone might have to say.

Angry red light from the setting sun shone through the bedroom blinds, but the room was filled with shadows and pools of darkness. I collapsed on the bed, exhausted. Suddenly a voice came from a far corner of the room.

"Nick. . . ."

I sprang up in the bed, startled out of my wits. I looked wildly around the room, but whoever was there was hiding in the shadows.

"Who's there? Who the fuck is it?"

Jennifer Joyner leaned forward out of the dark corner into a shaft of red light.

"It's me," she said. "Jennifer."

I was on my feet now. "Jennifer? You scared the piss out of me."

"Sorry. I fell asleep in the chair and didn't hear you come in."

"How'd you get into the house?"

"You loaned me a key when you wanted me to meet you here two weeks ago, remember?"

I sat on the edge of the bed and tried to clear my head. She was right. I had been working late a couple of weeks earlier and she had dropped by the set. She had said the right things to get me in the mood and I had told her to wait for me in my bed. I had given her a spare key to get in, something I almost never do for anyone, and I had forgotten to ask for it back. She had probably taken it as some mild sign of commitment. We had both made mistakes.

"I forgot," I muttered.

"You're pretty jumpy."

"I'm in a lot of trouble, Jenn."

"No kidding. I had to sneak around to the beach entrance to keep from getting plastered all over the front page tomorrow."

"You didn't have to come by at all."

"I wanted to."

Jennifer got up and crossed to the bed and sat beside me. She put her arms around my shoulders for comfort. It was a strange move, but I didn't pull away from her. She smelled good and felt even better.

"I spoke with Mark Pecchia," she said. "He wasn't very communicative. He's pretty angry."

"Who isn't?" I responded.

"I went to his set. He was in the middle of shooting another one of his black leather, rock and roll fantasies. Lots of smoke, girls, and guitars. He seemed kind of hyper. Maybe he's back on the blow."

"So what did he say, exactly?"

"He was pissed. He thinks you killed a friend of his. You met her at his party so he feels responsible. I told him you could never kill anyone and he told me to 'wake up and smell the espresso.' He said anyone who survived in show business *was* a killer already. That it's a natural instinct. He said you just took the symbolism to its logical conclusion. He wasn't in the mood to say much more. He was pretty rude."

I laughed. "There seems to be a lot of that going around."

"What's this all about, Nick?"

"I don't know. I don't know. I think I've been set up by someone, but I don't know why and I don't know who. What I *do* know is that I am into shit up to my eyebrows and no one believes I'm innocent."

"*I* believe you," Jennifer said.

I looked at her face. She returned the look with compassion.

"I know you couldn't do anything like that," she said. "I believed what I told Mark."

She gave my shoulders a squeeze. It didn't cheer me up. If anything it made me feel gloomier. Jennifer was so blind. For all she knew I *could* have been the killer. Hell, for all *I* knew, I was. The hours after I passed out with Candice Bishop were a complete blank. Even I was beginning to doubt myself. Could I have suffered some kind of psychotic blackout and done the horrible deed after all? What if I *was* guilty?

"You trust too much," I said. "At the right time anyone is capable of anything."

Jennifer withdrew a little. She seemed suddenly frightened, as if she thought I was trying to confess to the murder. But I didn't do it. I couldn't have blanked out that completely. I had to believe I was innocent. I didn't want to lose Jennifer's trust, either. I needed someone on my side and there weren't a lot of volunteers for the job.

"But this isn't one of those times," I said, trying to regain her confidence. "I didn't kill that girl. The last time I saw her she was very much alive."

This seemed to sting Jennifer deeply. "I bet," she said bitterly. It was almost as if she'd rather have me kill another woman than sleep with her.

"I'm sorry if I hurt you, Jenn. I'm so fucked up I don't know what I'm saying anymore. My entire life has been turned upside down. But you've stuck with me when nobody else would. You're a friend. A good friend."

I leaned over and gave her a soft kiss on the cheek. She was visibly moved by the simple gesture.

"Why, Nick. . . . Maybe there *is* a human being in there after all."

I involuntarily blushed at my show of affection. My wall had briefly dropped for someone. Or at least it had torn away a little. Jennifer returned a kiss, but this time on the lips, tender at first, then turning more passionate. She slowly pushed me back onto the bed, our lips never parting. I slid my pants off and removed her panties. I still had my shirt on and she was still wearing a red blouse and a black wraparound skirt. I decided to leave them on her, for now.

Jennifer positioned herself on top of me and we made contact. I slipped into her like we were two interlocking pieces of a combustion machine. Foreplay was nonexistent. We got right down to it. I slid my hands under her blouse and unsnapped the front of her bra. I freed her breasts and caressed them appreciatively. Her nipples were little rocks. She slid back and forth rhythmically on top of me. She pulled her skirt up and began moving faster and faster. I grabbed the sides of her hips and lifted her up and down. She was really burning now.

"Jeeeeesus . . . Christ," she moaned. "I'm coming . . . I'm coming!"

She pumped and slid along my cock, using it like her own private fuck tool. She was about to set a land speed record for us. She had never come this quickly before. It usually took quite a while to break through her cynicism.

I suddenly found myself straining to enjoy the experience. Maybe even straining to stay interested at all. Something had happened to me during my encounter with Candice Bishop. Another layer of callus had built up on my sexuality. Another jaded memory to distance me from normal pleasures.

Jennifer looked deep into my eyes and I tried to appear involved and intense. Suddenly her entire body began to shudder and shake with orgasm. She gasped, as if fatally stabbed.

"Oh God . . . oh God . . . ," she repeated over and over like some horny mantra.

I strained to remain fully erect. Something suddenly triggered a memory in my head. The way Jennifer moved her hair briefly reminded me of Candice Bishop. I could feel my interest swell noticeably. Jennifer climaxed and collapsed on top of me. She panted for a few moments before she could speak.

"Whew," she said. "Amazing what a kind word can do."

I slid out from under Jennifer. She started to roll over onto her side, thinking we were finished, but I grabbed her hips and kept them elevated.

"What are you doing?" she asked.

I flipped her skirt up off her rear end and positioned myself behind her.

"What's it look like?"

"Oh."

I pressed my pelvis against her buttocks.

"Careful. . . . Watch your aim," she said. I slipped into her vagina. She wasn't ready for anything rougher.

I flashed on Candice, tied down in a similar position under me, begging to be pushed over the edge.

I began pumping away at Jennifer from behind. She was still sensitive from her recent orgasm.

"Easy, Nick, easy . . . give a girl a chance to breathe."

I didn't hear her. I leaned my head back, remembering Candice as I thrust into Jennifer savagely. As I replayed my night with Candice in my head I relived it through Jennifer's body. My needs had been expanded by my experience. Jennifer, unaccustomed or unready for my sexual assault, experienced pleasure/pain similar to that which Candice craved.

"Goddamn," she stammered. "I don't believe it . . . I'm coming . . . again."

I could feel her tightening and drenching herself. I pressed into her as deeply as I could and let loose as well. Jennifer and I climaxed simultaneously for what seemed like a lifetime. We both went delirious. We kept grinding away at each other, trying to drain every last drop from our genitals, trying to meld our bodies at the point of contact. Finally we gave up in a moment of existential agony that reminded us we were actually two separate creatures, that we could never truly be one. I collapsed on her back and she rolled over onto her side. We were both soaked with sweat and come. I was tired, but I still hadn't gotten what I really needed out of the encounter. I wasn't satisfied. Maybe I never would be satisfied again.

———

Nick worked a box of paper clips on me one night and I thought I was with the fucking Marquis de Sade. That's what I like about him: his sense of the perverse.

—Jennifer Joyner

———

5

It took ten minutes before I felt like moving again. Jennifer was still facedown on the bed, half asleep, covered in a cold sweat. I put on a black robe and went downstairs for a glass of water. Night had fallen over the ocean, turning it cold and gray.

I brought the ice water back upstairs and touched Jennifer's back with the frosty glass. She spun around in shock from the sensation.

"Ouch," she said as she took the glass. "Thanks."

Jennifer sipped the water. I sat down on the bed and propped myself up against the headboard.

"Well, looks like I'm going to have to drop out of the triathlon," Jennifer said. "Unless they'll let me use a wheelchair. Christ, what got into you? I haven't been fucked like that since college."

I didn't really hear her. I was brooding, off in another

world. Jennifer shrugged off my indifference, rolled over, picked up the TV remote control, and turned on the tube. She began flipping through the channels. Violence and sex. Sex and violence. And that was just the networks. PBS was running a documentary about Nazi concentration camps.

Jennifer stopped on CNN. They were issuing an update on the hot young actor's overdose at The Crisis Center Sunday morning. There was actually no new information, but they felt obliged to keep the station on the air so they were continuing the speculation. Muckraking pays well. This was followed by a three-minute update on the latest Michael Jackson sex scandal. Then the latest "alleged Hollywood madam," Lise Rattinoff, picked up another three minutes of infamy. She was now selling designer satin sheets à la Heidi Fleiss while awaiting trial, and the media was giving her plenty of free commercial airtime. Jennifer took it all in hungrily and when the news switched to politics she began channel-surfing again. She was clicking through the airwaves so quickly I didn't think she could possibly tell what she was passing. Something caught Jennifer's eye and she went back a few channels. She landed on MTV, the rock video station.

"Here's one of Mark's videos," she said. "You can't watch this station for more than ten minutes without seeing one."

I shook the cobwebs from my head and looked at the screen. Black-leather-clad women with huge breasts were running long razor blade–like fingernails across the chest of a stringy-haired hard rocker sprawled out on the floor of a large, empty room, playing his guitar. Blood dripped profusely from the scratches. It was part *Nightmare on Elm Street,* part *Penthouse* fantasy. But there was something about the video that was even more familiar than the pop culture references. The location. . . .

"I know that place," I said to Jennifer.

"What?"

"I was there. I was at a place that looked just like that today. A warehouse owned by a freak named Nate Boritzer."

"What did you see Nate Boritzer for?" Jennifer asked. "You know him?"

"Everybody does. A lot of the guys shoot at his warehouse. It's a popular space. It's cheap and it's on the beach. He's also a dealer, so it's doubly convenient."

"A drug dealer?"

"Well, he sure doesn't sell Hondas."

"Does Mark Pecchia buy from him?" I asked.

"I don't know. . . . Probably. Nate hangs around Mark a lot. Mark's a good connection. Nate was at the party."

I squinted, trying to force the pieces into place. "He was? I don't remember seeing him."

"He showed up late. You were probably busy right here with your 'friend' by the time he got there."

There was still some bitterness about my dalliance in Jennifer's tone. I tried to let it pass.

"How late did he stay?"

"I don't know. I left pretty soon after he showed up."

Now it was my turn to discuss fidelity.

"Who'd *you* go home with?" I asked.

Jennifer didn't answer for a moment. She was caught with her double standard in her mouth. Finally she just gave a little laugh and confessed, "You're not the only one who knows how to make friends."

"I know."

We shared a moment of ennui. I think we were both trying to figure out what the hell we were doing with our lives. What *were* our lives anyway? A series of empty sexual encounters punctuated with flurries of work. The moment of introspection passed quickly.

"I got the feeling Nate wasn't going to stay long," Jennifer said. "I think he and Mark were going to go out and score some coke."

The wheels were starting to turn.

I got up and walked out onto my deck. I could hear the ocean crashing on the beach, but the night and the ash in the air had enveloped the distant lights of the city. Somewhere offshore a foghorn sounded, signaling that a marine layer was moving toward the coast. The foliage would get some much needed moisture tonight. Maybe nature would save Southern California from being burned to the ground. And maybe I was going to find a way to save myself from the dark forces that had been surrounding me.

PART XII

Don't panic.
    —Dale Holiday

1

I woke up around eleven the next morning. I felt terrific. Well rested and clearheaded. Jennifer was gone. I assumed she wasn't out in the Dumpster. I slipped on my robe and stepped out onto the deck for a smoke. The sky was clear and the wind was hot. The Santa Anas had returned with a vengeance. I took two puffs from the cigarette, then put it out. I'd be able to breathe enough hot air today.

The phone rang. I felt so good that I picked it up, forgetting about all the people I *didn't* want to speak to. It was Dale Holiday.

"Bad news on the neighbor front, Nick. Teddy Vincent was in Vancouver shooting a Roger Corman movie the night of the murder. He was definitely there and working when the thing went down. He got back two days later."

I could feel my heart sink. "What about Momberg?" I asked.

"He was working, too. Logged off around eleven. Had the next morning off, but I've got a source that places him at the Mondrian hotel with a couple of starlets from two A.M. till checkout Saturday afternoon. Seems he went to a wrap party at the Roxy and got himself lucky with the Doublemint twins."

"You get a lot done before lunchtime."

"I get up early."

"Doesn't look good, does it?"

"Don't panic. I've just begun to snoop. I'm going after this character Angelo next. He's a hustler. He's been in the skin flicks too. He was parlaying his relationship with the Bishop girl to get parts. Looks like he started cheating on her when her usefulness wore thin, but he still expected her to be loyal to him. They had a number of public rows in the last couple months. He fits the profile of jealous lover. Makes a good suspect."

"That's what you said about Teddy Vincent."

"Hey, that was yesterday."

"Right."

"Keep your chin up, but watch your back. That body may have been left in your Dumpster out of convenience or as a not-so-subtle attempt to frame you. We don't know. If you *have* been set up, whoever is behind it may not be done with you yet."

"You think I could be in danger?"

"Aren't we all?"

"Yeah, I guess so."

I hung up. The gloom descended again.

I went downstairs to get the mail. It was on the floor at the base of the front door. I picked up a handful of envelopes and a small package.

I walked through the house, flipping through the envelopes. Bills and junk mail. Nothing interesting. I looked at the package. Typed labels. Beverly Hills postmark. The return address in the upper left corner read simply "Karma City Central."

I sat the envelopes down on the bar and tore open the package. Inside I found a videotape and a plain white card with the words "You're my inspiration" typed on it. I stared at the card and the videotape. Then I noticed that my hands were shaking.

I went upstairs and slipped the tape into my VCR, turned on the television, and hit Play.

There were the standard color bars and tone that indicated that a professional duplicating machine had turned out the tape. Then an image popped on. An image I had never actually seen before, yet I recognized immediately. A girl was having sex on a bed with two men. Two men I hadn't seen in over a decade. The girl was young. Eighteen, maybe nineteen. She had curly black hair down to her shoulders, almond-shaped eyes, and thin lips. She appeared to be enjoying herself—at first. Then the sex got a little rougher. She stayed in the game, but she did not look happy about it. They rolled her flat on her back and one of the men fucked her while the other guy received a semi-forced blow job, twisting her neck in a very awkward and uncomfortable fashion. The men banged away at the girl from both ends of her body and climaxed simultaneously. As they pulled away from her she appeared limp. Her eyes were vacant. After a few seconds one of the men came back into frame and shook the girl. She did not respond. He shook her harder and she fell off the bed to the floor. The camera jumped and tilted wildly and suddenly the picture was gone. It was over.

I had never actually seen this film before, but I had witnessed the event. I had been looking through the viewfinder

of the camera when it all went down. This was the accidental snuff film that had sent me scurrying from the country over
a decade ago. I didn't even know that the negative had been
developed and copies printed. I had abandoned the set immediately after the girl died, leaving everything with Matty
and George, the two guys who had hired me. The two guys
who had sex with the girl in the film, breaking her neck and
smothering her to death in a moment of uncontrollable lust.
How and why this film had been transferred to tape and sent
to me was a mystery. Who was dredging up my past and trying to shove it down my throat? I felt my stomach start to boil.

Another picture popped onto the screen. The image was
cheap looking, obviously shot directly on video. A beautiful
sunset on the sea. I slowly realized it was only a painted backdrop as the camera pulled back to reveal Candice Bishop in
the foreground. She was scantily clad in torn designer rags.
Her arms and legs were stretched out and tied to two hori-
zontal poles that might have been broomsticks. It made her
body look like an X. She had a ball gag strapped in her mouth
and there was a rope tied to the middle of her arm pole that
extended into the air offscreen, obviously hooked to a ceiling
pulley to keep her on her feet. Cheap Muzak set the scene.
Something you might hear on an elevator in an insane asy-
lum. It was creepy.

A man entered the frame. He wore only a leather mask and
a jockstrap. A machete was strapped to his waist. The man
had roughly my coloring and build, and hair as I. He circled
Candice a few times, studying her like a hyena would survey
a piece of meat. Then he stopped behind her and looked
down at her ass. He pulled his jockstrap to the side and
rubbed his penis against her until it got hard. He pulled a
black French tickler condom lined with angry plastic studs

out of his jockstrap and slipped it over his cock. He reached around, tore what was left of Candice's top off, and mauled her breasts with both hands as he started pumping into her from the rear. Candice didn't look frightened. She actually appeared to be enjoying herself. I staggered back a few feet, my jaw hanging loose.

The man pounded away at Candice Bishop. She was really starting to get into it now, pushing her buttocks against him as hard as she could. I looked at the card in my hand, the words typed so simply there. *You're my inspiration.*

The man was done behind Candice. He stepped in front of her and lowered the control rope so that she was bent very far forward, as if she could perform oral sex on him if he removed her gag. But the man didn't remove Candice's gag. Instead he pulled the machete from its sheath on his waist and taunted her with it, touching her on her shoulders, her breasts, her ass. He straightened her up again and teased the blade around her vagina, tracing lips and pubic hair. And then I saw it. A cigarette burn just above her pubic area. I realized fully what this tape was, when it was shot, what was about to happen. These were going to be the last seconds of Candice Bishop's life. This was a snuff film, shot the night she died, within hours of the time she was with me.

The man lowered Candice into the bent position again. Candice looked up at him curiously. It became obvious, even to her, what he really had in mind. She started to panic. She struggled, but couldn't move much. She tried to scream, but the gag was too tight. All the devices of masochistic pleasure had suddenly taken on lethal implications. She had allowed herself to be trapped into submission and silence by these bastards and now they could do anything they wanted to do to her without being heard.

The man stood in front of Candice as if trying to decide
something. Candy looked off-camera, pleading with someone
there with her eyes. The masked man looked off-camera as
well, receiving instructions. Whatever was said totally freaked
Candice out. She started flailing at her bonds like a frightened
bull in a slaughterhouse, but it was to no avail. She was
trapped. Tears were now streaming down her face. Her eyes
were wide with terror. The man in the mask lifted the machete over his head.

I looked down at the card in my hand to avoid seeing what
I knew was going to happen. Mark Pecchia's words at the
party came back to me: *"You're the best there is, Nick. . . ."*

Out of the corner of my eye I saw the man swing down hard
with the machete.

"You're my inspiration." Mark Pecchia's words, repeated
on the otherwise blank calling card. A coded confession that
would never hold up in court. Not in a million fucking years.
I crushed the card in my hand and stared through tears at
the image on the monitor. Candice Bishop had been decap-
itated, on camera, by a man in a mask whose body could easily double for mine. The frame around me was clear now, the
reasons still a blur. Someone had murdered a girl and wanted
me to burn for it. Not just burn, but suffer slowly as well. The
who had all but been answered. The next question was *why?*

2

I called Dale Holiday's office, but he wasn't in. I wasn't even
sure what I was going to tell him. I thought I had some answers, but they led to more questions. It was certainly no full
vindication on my part. What I really had in my possession

was incriminating evidence that could send me to the gas chamber if it was interpreted against my favor.

I dressed quickly and hauled ass in the Lamborghini toward Beverly Hills. I was looking to break the sound barrier. As I went up Sunset Boulevard I could see a giant plume of reddish brown smoke rising over the mountains to the north. I turned on the radio and discovered that arsonists had struck again and a raging fire was racing toward Malibu all the way from Calabasas. I didn't have time to worry about it. I had my own fire to put out.

I made Beverly Hills in record time. I ripped up Benedict Canyon and screeched to a halt sideways in front of Mark Pecchia's driveway. There were a number of expensive cars and a couple of junkers parked there. I blocked them completely with my car. No one was getting out of here until this thing was over.

I went to the front door and was met by a behemoth of a man whom I recognized as Jerry Pendrell, an ex-linebacker for the Raiders who had blown out his knee in his second year with the team. He must have blown his money up his nose too, because he was working as Mark Pecchia's bodyguard now.

"Where is he?" I asked.

"I have to search you," Jerry said.

"Bullshit."

"Then you have to leave."

I looked Jerry Pendrell over. He was still a monster, fucked up knee and all. It wouldn't be worth the fight even if I could take him, which was highly unlikely. I turned and faced the wall.

"Knock yourself out," I said.

Jerry frisked me. He wasn't gentle about it. He checked my chest and crotch areas the most thoroughly. I got the feeling he was more interested in any recording devices I might have on me than weapons. Either that or he was a closet fag, like half the NFL.

Satisfied, Jerry led me through the house and out the sliding glass doors in the back. A steep hill led down to the swimming pool and the tennis court. We rode down the mountainside in a big blue metal tram like we were at Magic Mountain.

Mark Pecchia sat by the swimming pool reading a copy of *Billboard* magazine. He was in swim trunks and a white terry cloth robe hung off his shoulders. A row of tall fir trees provided shade from the sun. The atmosphere was quite pleasant. A man sat on the edge of a lounge chair five feet away from Mark Pecchia. The man was not as large as Jerry Pendrell, but he looked meaner. He was picking his teeth with a matchstick and staring into the swimming pool as if he were angry at it for being so clear and blue. Since when did rock video directors need bodyguards?

Mark Pecchia took no notice as Jerry Pendrell and I approached. He simply turned a page of his magazine and kept reading.

"How's it going, bud?" Pecchia asked without looking up from *Billboard*.

"You know why I'm here," I said, trying to sound intimidating.

"I'm not a mind reader," Pecchia said through a thin smile.

"You set me up. You killed that girl and you set me up."

Pecchia finally looked up from his magazine. "I assume you're talking about Candice Bishop. From what I read in the papers, *you* killed her."

I paced nervously in front of him. His words and attitude were as good as a confession. To me at least. The authorities would need a hell of a lot more.

"Why? Why me?" I stuttered, losing some of my bravado.

"Is that all you ever think about? Yourself?" Pecchia asked. "What about *her*? Why don't you ask 'Why her?' Because the truth is, you don't give a fuck about anyone but yourself."

I stared at him, trying to figure out what the hell this game was all about.

Mark Pecchia got up and walked over to the wet bar on the side of the pool. He began rolling a joint culled from a giant bag of what looked to be high-grade pot.

"Yeah," he said. "You killed that girl, all right. You may not have chopped her head off yourself, but you killed her, just as sure as you killed the other one ten years ago."

My face grew ashen. *How could he know?* But of course he did. He had assembled the two tapes.

"What the hell are you talking about?" I asked nervously.

"Need me to spell it out?" Pecchia asked as he lit the joint.

"I guess you better."

"It takes more than a few years dicking around in Europe to clean a slate as dirty as yours. Hit?"

He offered me the joint. I was in a daze, but I waved him away. He shrugged and walked back to his chair and sat in the lotus position. The bodyguards had no reaction to any of this. They were like big, ugly mannequins.

"You must've really thought you were hot shit when you hit the big time and no one showed up to nail you," Pecchia continued. "Did you really think you were going to get away with murder like that?"

"I didn't kill anybody! Not then and not now!"

"That's what the other guys said, but here we have it: Dead

girls everywhere and no murderers in the whole fucking town. Weird, huh?"

"You did it, you crazy bastard. You killed Candice Bishop."

"No, Nicky, baby. You killed her the moment you took her home with you. And now you're going to fry for it. You're finished. End of story. It's just a matter of time now before they reel you in. Ever been fucked in the ass, Nick? Those big boys are gonna dig your little white cheeks in jail. Hope you catch as well as you pitch."

I rushed toward Pecchia. The seated bodyguard stuck his foot out and tripped me. Jerry Pendrell intercepted the pass. He punched me in the gut, knocking the wind out of me. I collapsed on the ground, trying desperately to breathe.

"How's it feel to be on the receiving end, Nicky?" Pecchia cackled. "Better get used to it. The niggers love white trash like you in the slammer."

"You sick fuck!" I wheezed. "You murdered that girl just to get back at me? For something I didn't even do? I'm gonna fucking kill you!" It must've seemed a very idle threat coming from a man who was trying to find his lungs on the ground in front of him.

"Get him out of here," Pecchia said to Jerry Pendrell. "The meeting is over."

Jerry picked me up by the collar and started to drag me toward the blue tram.

"You're not going to get away with this!" I said to Pecchia. "I'll tell the cops everything! I'll show them the video! You're the one who's going to fry!"

Jerry slammed my head against the door frame of the metal tram, stunning me into silence. He pulled me onto the platform of the tram and hit the Up button. The cable car began the slow crawl back up the hill toward the house, clicking loudly as it went. Going uphill was a much bigger strain on the motor than coming down had been.

Mark Pecchia stood up and watched us ascend.

"Go ahead," he said. "Show them the video. That's why I sent it to you. Try to explain it to the cops. They'll never believe you, Nick! You're a well-known pornographer with aliases. A very suspicious character. *I'm* an artist, respected everywhere. The evidence is all stacked against you. *You* fucked her that night, I didn't. You've got possession of the video, I don't. Who do you think they're going to believe? You look so set up, you *have* to be guilty." Pecchia laughed sourly. There was great hatred in his voice.

I was in so much pain, I couldn't give him an answer even if I had one. I wouldn't have dared anyway. Not with an ex-linebacker's hand around my throat. I just rode silently with Jerry Pendrell toward the top of the hill.

Mark Pecchia saluted me and clicked his bare heels together with a laugh. "Enjoy the ride up, Nick!" he said. "You won't be moving in that direction again for a long, long time. See ya, buddy."

I stared down at Pecchia with anger in my eyes and nausea in the pit of my stomach. The tram reached the top of the hill. Pendrell shoved me through the swinging doors toward the house. He held me firmly by the back of the neck as we went through the house as if he were afraid I'd go crazy and break something. He tossed me out the front door like I was some bar drunk who had pissed off the management. I landed on my knees first, then my palms.

"Don't fucking come back, scumbag!" Pendrell yelled.

I got up and dusted myself off. My pants were torn and my hands and knees were bleeding. I stared at Jerry Pendrell as I got into my car. His boss had practically confessed to a mur-

der in front of him, yet *I* was the scumbag. I could tell I was
in Beverly Hills.

———

*I had nothing against him personally. I didn't really
even know him. But stuff had happened a long time ago
and he was responsible. No matter what he says, he was
responsible.*

—Mark Pecchia

———

PART XIII

It wasn't the first time they used that room.

—Nate Boritzer

1

Jim Morrison was locked in his "Mr. Mojo Risin' " mantra in "L.A. Woman" as I sped out of Beverly Hills. I had jammed the tape back in, not wanting to hear the barrage of news stories about the Malibu fires that were flooding the airwaves. They had already dubbed this current blaze "Firestorm II." They had *sequelized* the fires.

I got Whitney on my car phone. The stage was dark today, so he was home. I told him what I needed. Fifteen minutes later I pulled into the parking garage of his apartment building in one of Hollywood's seedier neighborhoods.

Whitney was waiting for me, leaning against the trunk of his '86 Camaro. I pulled up in the slot beside him and got out. We stared at each other for a moment, then Whitney turned and popped open the trunk of his car, revealing a small arsenal of pistols and assault rifles laid out and strapped down on the floor of the compartment.

"Choose careful, dude," Whitney said with a grin.

"Where the fuck did you get all this?" I asked.

187

"You don't think I can afford to live on what you guys pay me, do you?"

I couldn't believe it. My camera assistant was a part-time gun dealer. This town was in serious trouble.

"Aren't you afraid of being searched by the cops?" I asked.

"Nah," Whitney said. "I'm white."

It seemed a naive attitude, but maybe he was right. Since the Rodney King incident and the riots, the cops in L.A. weren't watching white folks as closely as they used to. The statistics just didn't call for it. They were getting as color-conscious as they were usually accused of being. That was probably one of the reasons Di Bacco was so keen on seeing me convicted. It would look good to put a white guy away. Especially a semi-famous one. It would be politically correct. They could wave my ass like a lily-white flag for the next three years every time some black attorney yelled "racist." Nail me and maybe the next O.J. would get convicted.

I studied the weapons in the trunk. Many of them were totally unfamiliar to me. I picked a 9mm Beretta. I had a girlfriend in Germany who had one just like it and we used to go target shooting once in a while. It was the only gun experience I ever had.

"Good choice," Whitney said. "It's clean. But it's also four bills."

I only had a little over two hundred bucks on me. I gave Whitney the two, kept some carrying cash, and told him I'd pay him the rest the following day.

"Make sure you're still around to pay me, boss," Whitney said.

"If I'm not, go into the office and take it out in camera equipment."

"You want some help, man?"
"No. This is my deal. I've got to play it out."
"It's your funeral."
"Probably."
Whitney shook my hand with the four-stage soul shake.
"No prisoners, boss. No prisoners."

2

I ripped back up Benedict Canyon, blowing the doors off all the other cars on the road. I screeched to a halt in front of Mark Pecchia's house. There weren't as many cars in the driveway as before. Someone had left. I hoped it was the bodyguards and not Mark Pecchia. Maybe they had been hired for the event only. Or maybe they were just very close acquaintances repaying favors or drug loans. It was doubtful, considering that Mark had as much as confessed to Candice's murder in front of them. No, they had to be in on the scheme as well. As I thought about it I realized that the guy sitting by the pool who tripped me could have been the masked man in the video. He was approximately my height, coloring, and build, although he looked like he was in somewhat better shape than me.

I got out of the car, carrying the Beretta low and in front of me. I went up to the front door and rapped on it with the pistol. There was no answer. I went through a maze of thick bushes and trees around to the rear of the house. I looked down the hill at the swimming pool and tennis courts. No one was there. I went to the sliding glass doors at the rear of the house and rapped on the glass with the pistol. Still no answer.

I slammed the edge of the Beretta against the glass door,

shattering it. Glass cascaded down in front of me. I turned away for a moment to shield my eyes from the flying shards. If there was an alarm it was silent or turned off. I stepped through the shattered doorway and made a very quick room-to-room search of the house. Vengeance would have to wait. Nobody was home. I had gone to all the trouble of purchasing a gun, like a proper Angeleno, and I had steeled myself for some good old-fashioned vengeance like they do in the movies, but I had been defeated by the simple fact that no one was home. The bad guys were always home for Clint Eastwood or Sly Stallone. It would have been comical if I was in a better state of mind, but I had the fever. I realized I was going down. I wasn't going to get out of this one this time. But I wanted to take Mark Pecchia with me. He'd never do time for Candice Bishop's murder. *I* would. I wanted to avenge myself as well as the poor girl they had used to get to me.

I had the who, and I had the how, what I still didn't know was the why. Why did Mark Pecchia hate me so? I didn't even know the guy. What did this have to do with what happened over ten years ago? How did he even know about that? What was the connection? My head was swimming with questions.

I considered sitting and waiting for Pecchia and his boys to return. There was a good chance that it would be the Beverly Hills Rent-a-Cops instead. I was willing to take the chance. Then an image came back to me in a flash and I suddenly realized that there was one person I had met who might have the answers I needed. Someone who knew about Candice Bishop's murder and had probably been there when it went down. Maybe he could even be frightened into a confession. See, there was one thing familiar in the Candice

Bishop snuff film that hadn't registered with me until now. The floor. The floor in the room where Candice was killed. The floor was splattered with various colors of old paint.

I got back into my car and roared down Benedict Canyon. I was heading for the beach.

3

It was almost dark by the time I got through traffic to Venice Beach. Parking was relatively easy this time. Everyone had headed home long ago. Huge clouds of smoke hung over Malibu to the north. The flames had gotten away from the firefighters and were now making the "firestorm" of a few days ago look tame by comparison. Half of Malibu was burning. Let it burn, I thought to myself. Let it all burn. Including *my* fucking house.

I kicked the front door of Nate Boritzer's warehouse open. Nate was sitting in a tall director's chair in the center of the big, empty room, a bottle of Bacardi 151 in one hand, a cigarette in the other. A single light from a bare bulb dangling loosely from the ceiling shone directly over his head, creating a halo effect around him. Dead cigarettes covered the floor around the chair. God knows how long he had been sitting there, drinking and smoking, letting that nonsense dance around in his head.

Nate Boritzer looked up at me and smiled. He either didn't notice or didn't care that I had a gun in my hand. He took a sip from the bottle and a puff from the cigarette. I crossed the room as quickly as I could without running. Another sip from the bottle and I was right in front of him.

I pistol-whipped the Bacardi bottle in mid-swig and it

shattered in Nate Boritzer's face. Nate looked startled as he fell backwards. The chair tipped over and he crashed to the floor.

I stood over Nate, aiming the pistol point-blank at his bleeding, glass-covered face.

"Now, fucker, you're going to talk," I said. "You're gonna get me out of this mess." I was all raw nerves and adrenaline. Very little reason was left in my head.

Nate tried to wipe glass and rum out of his eyes. He finally comprehended what had just happened to him.

"Aaasssshooollle!" he yelled. It was a deep, guttural yell. He managed to stretch the word out for a good seven seconds.

I stomped Nate Boritzer in the nuts to distribute his pain more evenly. The action sent a wave of relief through me. I felt like kicking the shit out of the little fuck; instead I simply bent forward and put the pistol to his cheek. With my free hand I pulled him closer by the collar of his dirty sweatshirt.

"Yeah, I'm an asshole," I said. "And so are you. Only difference is, you're about to be a *dead* asshole."

I chambered a shell in the gun.

"Don't do it," he yelled. "Don't, man!" Either he believed I meant business or he thought I might make a mistake handling the gun and shoot him by accident. Either way he was scared.

"Why not?" I asked. "Everything's shit, right? I'm just gonna put you out of your misery!"

"No, no, c'mon, you don't want to kill anybody!"

"I've already killed two women, right? What's one more?"

I jammed the barrel of the gun into Nate's crotch and shook him by the collar.

"I can't do anything!" he screamed. "It's too late!"

"Then you're gonna die."

I jabbed him in the chest with the gun. Nate was shaking like crazy.

"See your buddy!" he said. "Your old partner. David . . . David Rink! He can help you!"

This got my attention. I backed the gun off a few inches.

"David Rink? What's he got to do with this?"

"Oh, man, c'mon. He shot the stuff."

My jaw dropped.

"He shot the snuff film?" I asked incredulously.

"Fuck, yes. They used my back room, but *he* shot it."

"Who else was there?"

"I don't know."

I pistol-whipped Nate in the face again. It opened up an old scar under his right eye. Blood trickled down and joined the tiny rivulets that were flowing from the glass cuts.

"I swear to God, I don't know," Nate whimpered. "I was zoned out that night. . . . I don't remember shit! But it wasn't the first time they used that room."

"They who?"

"You know. Mark and David."

"They've . . . killed other girls?"

"Of course. You think they did all this just for you? You're vain. They've got a business, man. Sort of a cultural exchange program, you know, a pound of flesh every now and then for a kilo of coke here and there. Those guys, they're in deep with some dudes from the south. You're just the cherry on top of it all this time."

"Why?"

"Ask Rink. He knows more than I do. He got me into this shit. I never wanted it. Never!"

"You're going to tell this whole story to the police."

Nate spit blood onto the floor. "Yeah, right," he said sarcastically.

I hit him in the face with the gun again. Nate's attitude adjusted properly. He tried to shake off the effects of the blow. He slumped a little, accepting his fate.

"Whatever you say," Nate mumbled.

"Let's go," I said.

I picked Nate up off the floor and shoved him toward the door. He staggered drunkenly all over the place. I kept hold of his arm with my free hand to control him. I opened the door. Nate started to step out. He suddenly half-turned, grabbed the door, and slammed it into my face. I fell backward and dropped the Beretta. Nate pulled the door shut, cackled like a madman, and hauled ass down the street.

I shook the pain off, picked up the gun, and rushed out onto the sidewalk. I pointed the gun at Nate Boritzer and fired twice. Nate was already out of range for my lousy aim. He cut a hard right and disappeared down an alley.

The street was suddenly alive with people yelling and screaming from their houses and apartments, things like "Someone's shooting," "Get my shotgun," and "Shut the fuck up out there."

I slowly became aware of what I was doing. I was standing in the middle of the street in Venice, California, firing a gun. I walked quickly to my car and threw the Beretta into the passenger seat. I climbed in and started the Lamborghini. I looked around at the surrounding houses. The braver residents were beginning to peer out their windows. I was more embarrassed than frightened.

People started coming out of their dwellings, staring at me. Some of them carried pistols and rifles. A few of them looked like they'd really like to get a chance to use their weapons. A man on a nearby porch aimed a pump shotgun at me.

"Don't move," he shouted. "I called nine-one-one."

I burned rubber out of there. The man with the shotgun yelled curses at me and fired into the air. He was absolutely civilized about the whole affair.

———

He was a crazy fuck. I knew it the first time I saw him. He had that look in his eyes. Like a hunted animal. A goddamn elk that's been shot. But that second time he came to see me he almost killed me. It felt good hitting him in the face with that door. He had it coming.

—Nate Boritzer

———

PART XIV

I think he's got a hard-on for dead women.

—David Rink

1

I drove without really knowing where I was going. The more I saw of the puzzle, the more questions I had. I was on autopilot as I sifted the information I had gathered through my brain. By the time I was actually paying attention to my surroundings I found myself driving the deserted, garbage-strewn streets of the warehouse district of downtown Los Angeles. Subconsciously, instinctively, I had gone home. Home to a place I had not seen in over a decade. The loft. The place where it all began.

I parked and looked up at the old three-story building, red-brick, dotted with plates connected to steel rods driven through the walls to hold the place together during earthquakes. It was a three-story job. David's loft occupied one complete corner of the bottom floor. The rest of the place housed garment manufacturing sweatshops where the wetbacks grunted out twelve-hour workdays and got paid for six. They were all closed now. No use flagging Immigration with a twenty-four-hour operation. No reason to get *greedy*.

The street was dead. An eerie silence pervaded the steel-

and-brick canyon. Not even bums liked to hang out in this neighborhood at night. There was no one to feed off except for the artists who occupied some of the lofts full-time. Most of them were poorer than the average homeless person. The only life to be seen came from the Santa Ana winds that gently blew loose paper and Styrofoam cups down the street. Even the Santa Anas were subdued in this ghost town.

A faint glow was in the window of the loft. As I got closer I could hear rock music filtering out from within the place. Jimmy Page's old supergroup, the Firm, was playing "Tear Down the Walls."

I tried the door to the loft. It was locked of course. I reached through the metal bars on the exterior of the door and smashed two of the middle jalousie windows. David Rink and I had glued them all shut eons ago, when we first leased the place. The building hadn't changed a bit in all that time. It was like looking at something out of a time capsule.

I reached through the metal bars and turned the lock on the doorknob. Back when we were partners David was notorious for forgetting to lock deadbolts and set alarms. He was incredibly lazy about things like that, no matter what kind of crime zone he lived in. He didn't like messing around with any more keys than he had to. We used to argue about the subject often. His pattern had held, but now I was glad he was so lackadaisical. The door swung open and I entered. No alarms, no hassles.

It was dark in the loft. The only illumination was coming from two neon signs, a standard-issue Heineken advert and a custom job that said "FUCK IT!" in red. The music was much louder now that I was inside. David had it up full blast. I could also hear a phone ringing somewhere in the loft, but it was too dark for me to see where it was located.

The loft was just large enough for a functional studio space and a couple of tiny offices. A homemade second floor stretched out over roughly one third of the room on the north side above the bathroom and the kitchenette in an attempt to maximize the space. I hit the light switch on the side of the door, but nothing came on. The bulb was burned out.

I was carrying the pistol, aiming it defensively in front of me, unsure whether David was here or not, whether he was alone or traveling with his own set of aging football players turned bodyguards. I didn't plan on getting slapped around again. I peered through the shadows and stepped cautiously toward the wooden ladder that led to the second floor. This was where David used to keep his part of the office and a cot for napping. I could only hope that he hadn't changed his basic floor plan. I climbed with one hand, holding the gun in front of me with the other.

I got to the second floor and it was even darker than it was downstairs. The neon glow didn't clear the landing. A few tiny lights could be seen on the stereo along the far wall, but the rest of the area was pitch-black. I could hear that the phone was up here, ringing on a desk somewhere in the darkness. I stared through the gloom at David's cot, trying to let my eyes adjust. It was too dark to tell for sure, but it looked like someone was sleeping there. I could hear traces of a slow, rhythmic breathing under the loud music.

I flipped a light switch on the wall. A standing halogen lamp came on in the corner of the room, filling the place with harsh white light. I looked over at the cot, but it was not a cot anymore. David had squeezed a four-poster bed up here, a morsel left over from his messy divorce. Maybe he had given the cot to Nate Boritzer.

David Rink was asleep in the bed, wrapped in a thick green

comforter, dead to the world, snoozing through noise, light, phones, whatever. His breathing was deep and slow. He looked like he was on tranquilizers of some sort.

I reached over and turned off the radio. I looked at his messy desk and saw why his answering machine hadn't picked up the phone. It was smashed to pieces on the floor next to the desk. I pulled the phone line out of the wall, killing the ringing, and tossed the phone next to the smashed answering machine. This did not wake David Rink.

I walked over to the bed and stood above David, the Beretta dangling from my arm at my side. I put my foot on the wooden frame of the bed and shook it slowly. Then harder. Then I kicked the shit out of it.

David woke with a start and looked up at me through heavy eyelids. He didn't appear shocked to see me.

"I could have had a party up here and you would have slept right through it," I said.

"That's the idea," he replied groggily.

"Why the fuck did you set me up?"

David rolled over and turned his back to me.

"Go away," he mumbled.

"What's wrong with you?"

"Tired . . ."

"Talk to me, David. I'm in a lot of trouble and you put me there. I want out."

"Nothing I can do."

He wasn't paying attention. I decided to resort to subtle threats.

"David, I've got a gun," I said calmly.

David chuckled. "So?"

I kicked the bed and yelled, "So get up and FUCKING TALK TO ME!"

"Can't we do this tomorrow?" he groaned.

"What are you on?"

"Just some pills . . . haven't been sleeping good."

"Join the club."

I reached over, grabbed David by the arms, and pulled him out from under the comforter. David was fully dressed in a wrinkled Armani suit. He had just crawled into bed without changing. He tried to shake me off, but I hoisted him to his feet.

"Goddamnit, Nick, leave me alone," he grumbled, not wanting to get fully conscious.

I shoved David down into a swivel chair at the desk.

"Not until I get what I want!" I yelled into his face, trying to startle him out of his fog.

David blinked repeatedly and rubbed his eyes. I shifted on my feet and felt the gun in my hand. My anger was making me nervous.

"What do you think I can do?" David asked, starting to come around.

"You killed that girl and pinned it on me. You can get me out of this whole mess."

"I can't. There's no way. And *I* didn't kill anybody."

"You were there. You shot that video. . . . YOU'RE RE-SPONSIBLE!"

"Like *you* were ten years ago?"

My face suddenly dropped. I slowly sat down on the edge of the bed.

"That was different," I said. "You know it was."

"How?"

"I didn't know they were going to do what they did. . . . *They* didn't even know. It was an accident. Things just got out of hand. I tried to stop them, but I didn't move fast enough."

"Yeah. . . . Well you moved plenty fast afterwards. While you were out making a name for yourself in Hamburg and Paris, I was here taking the rap for that murder."

"What rap? Nobody ever got caught."

"Not by the cops."

"What are you talking about?"

"We were *partners,* Nick. You ran."

"What happened?"

"I belong to those assholes, now."

"Who?"

"*My* bosses. . . . *Her* family. . . ."

"WHAT THE FUCK ARE YOU TALKING ABOUT?"

"It was that chick . . . that chick you and Matty snuffed . . . she was *connected.*"

I was finally catching on. I felt myself sinking deeper into the quagmire. Ten years of nightmares flushed my face.

"The mob?" I asked.

"Yeah. She was the niece of some mafioso bigwig from New York. She was just doing porn to get back at her family or some shit like that. She didn't expect to get killed. When the boys finally figured out what had happened they came down on me hard."

"But you had nothing to do with it. You weren't even there."

"I was your *partner.* They traced you to me."

"What did they do?"

"They hurt me bad. And when I got out of the hospital, I was ruined. They own my ass, lock, stock, and barrel. They wanted in on the West Coast porn trade, but they wanted to keep a low profile. They decided to use me as a front man for them. That's all I am. Just a front. A beard. The guy who will take the fall if Fantasy City ever gets busted. I do what they want or I don't do anything."

"Why don't you take off?"

"Where to . . . South America? Or maybe Europe, like you?"

"Why not?"

"I don't like to run, and even if I did, I wouldn't get far from these guys."

"So you kill innocent women instead. . . . You got balls. You make me want to puke."

"That's Mark's thing. The guys in New York don't know anything about it."

"Then why do you do it?" I asked.

"I take my orders from him."

"Pecchia's mob-connected?"

"Fuck, yes. He loves doing his little rock videos but he's also a major L.A. conduit between Colombia and New York for the white stuff. The director gig is the perfect cover and the perfect networking tool. He's considered big time in New York. Kind of a freak, but big time. That girl you guys wasted? She was his *sister.*"

I didn't think my jaw could get much lower, but it managed to drop another two feet.

"This is crazy. This can't be happening. . . . It doesn't make any sense."

"Make sense? If you wanted things to make sense you should have never come back to L.A."

"This guy's trying to get revenge on me for being involved with something that I had no control over. I didn't plan anything. It was just supposed to be a porn loop. No one was supposed to get hurt! It was Matty and that maniac George.

They lost it and smothered that girl while I was rolling the camera. They didn't mean to do it. They just lost control and got carried away. We didn't even know she was dead until we stopped filming. It was just a stupid accident."

"That's not the way they saw it back in New York," David said. "Somehow prints of the film got out; Matty and George must've printed the fucker. It circulated in the underground for a couple of years before one of the mob guys saw it. They'd been looking for the girl for years. Needless to say, the shit hit the proverbial fan. Matty and George had moved operations to the Apple trying to stay away from L.A. in case anyone came looking for the girl. They had no idea they had moved out of the frying pan, into the fire."

"I still don't see how all that led up to Candice Bishop's murder."

"Mark was obsessed. For years he was obsessed with the whole thing. He used to talk about how it must've been for the guys who were in that room when his sister got snuffed. How the bastards must've got off on it. He had a copy of the film and he'd watch it over and over again. He was obsessed . . . and finally he did something about it. He acted out his obsession. Candice wasn't the first, but she was becoming an embarrassment to the Community and she had to go. Whenever some chick crossed Mark or his people in a way that couldn't be dealt with cleanly, she became a candidate for the warehouse. He calls it 'Justice Therapy.' I think he's got a hard-on for dead women."

"The guy's a fucking nutcase."

"I guess it's all a matter of perspective. Some would say he's just a good businessman. He does well with the snuffs. He's got worldwide distribution. He's even on the Internet. You wouldn't believe how much demand there is for this kind of thing in the underground."

"If the other guys in the business find out what you're doing, you'll disappear—both of you—no matter what kind of muscle is backing Pecchia."

"I warned Mark that there could be ramifications," David said. "He wasn't concerned."

"Then he's not as smart as he thinks he is. You know those guys won't tolerate any pissing in the pond. It's bad for business." When the big wigs in porn find out someone's moving kiddie porn or snuff films they either report them to the FBI or handle it on their own. When shit like that floats around it makes them all look bad. They were willing to get as rough as it took to keep the air clean.

"Mark Pecchia's health is the last thing that should be on your mind," David said.

"How did he find me?" I asked.

"Actually, *I* found you. I saw that piece they did on slick-dick ad shooters on *Entertainment Tonight* a few months ago. You do a good interview for a guy who's supposed to be on the lam. Smooth move."

A freelance documentary crew had invaded one of my outdoor locations and I had given them a few sentences to make them go away, trying not to arouse any kind of suspicion. The fuckers had sold the footage to *ET.* Lou had been thrilled with the publicity at the time. Of course *I* was horrified, but I soon forgot all about it. The media dogs had struck again. I had caught my dick in the fame wringer. I had never wanted it, it just happened.

"I was only on the screen for twenty seconds," I said. "How did you recognize me?"

"You haven't changed *that* much," he replied.

I paced nervously in front of David Rink. He was starting to smile, enjoying the show.

"I'm not taking the rap for you sick bastards!" I said.

"You've got no choice." David's upper lip curled with arrogant satisfaction. "The cops are in charge now. Nothing you tell them will change anything. They've got what they need and there's no way you can stop them."

"*You* can stop them. You can tell them the truth."

David got up and walked over to the wooden banister. He looked down into the studio below, *our* old studio, where our careers began two decades ago, and shook his head.

"No way in fucking hell," he said.

David seemed *glad* to see me in this jam. I was willing to bet they didn't have to twist his arm to get him to help set me up. He obviously blamed me for his last ten years of enslavement. All his braggadocio at Fantasy City took on tragic meaning in this light. It had all been a paint job. He had nothing. His life was nothing. He was exactly where he was a decade ago. Worse. What little he had then didn't even belong to him now. He had been completely stripped of his manhood and left as a shell, a figurehead, without true wealth or power. Only the illusion. The veneer. He was a patsy. A failure, all the way around. I should have felt some form of sympathy for him, but I didn't. I should have felt some twinge of guilt or responsibility for his sorry excuse of an existence, but I couldn't. There was always a way out if you really wanted it, as long as you didn't give up hope. His slavery was at least *partially* voluntary. I'm sure he *liked* being the big honcho at Fantasy City, even if it was a front. He still got to live and act like a king. It was the closest thing to success he would ex-

perience in this lifetime. He had made his pact with the devil
just as surely as I had.

I walked over and faced David Rink eye to eye.

"Tell them, David," I said. "Tell the police the truth."

"And take the heat for you again?" he asked. "Not this
time, Chief."

"You didn't have to take it the first time."

"They *killed* Matty and George. They put me in the hospital just for *knowing* you. If I had been in the room with
you assholes when it went down they would've killed me
too."

"Why haven't they killed *me?*"

"They would have if they could have found you back then.
But it's been more than ten years. Mark's softened on the
whole business. Thing's are different now. His uncle died a
couple of years ago. The heat died with him. Mark didn't even
tell the boys in New York that he found you. Don't get me
wrong, he still wanted revenge, he just thought the law should
handle the situation. Irony or some shit. I don't know what's
in his head. The guy's got a weird sense of humor."

"He's a real comedian."

"You been kind of funny yourself."

"This is the most fucked thing I've ever seen."

"You should'a never gone off to scab with Matty."

"I needed the money. We weren't making enough and you
were stuffing more than your share up your nose. Or did you
forget that part of the story?"

David sized me up.

"You're right. What's the difference? You're a big man now."

David and I stared each other down. A decade of rage was
building in both of us.

"You always were a loser, David," I said. "Nothing's changed."

"*You're* the one who's going to jail."

"We'll see about that."

"Nothing you can do about it."

"I'll do whatever it takes."

"Maybe you can run . . . again."

"Fuck you," I said.

"No. Fuck YOU!"

David growled like a rabid coyote and lunged at me. He slammed me back against the wall and punched me in the stomach. He was totally alert now. No sign of the drugged out character he was a few minutes earlier. He punched me in the stomach again and my gun went flying over the rail onto the floor below.

David hit me in the face with his forearm. I took it, then shoved him back with the palms of my hands. David staggered back a few feet. I pushed myself off the wall and hit him hard in the chest with my palms again, trying to give myself space so I could catch my breath.

David's heel caught against the bottom of the four-poster bed and he was propelled backwards. He crashed into the wooden railing and it splintered. For a moment I thought it would hold, but his weight was too much for the rickety construction. We had built it ourselves almost twenty years ago and it was not designed to take this kind of punishment. As I reached out for him, the wood gave and David disappeared over the side. He fell twenty-five feet and landed on a collection of lamps, tripods, and other photographic equipment that was being stored on the first floor.

I went to the broken rail and looked down. David was tangled in a pile of twisted metal and shattered glass. I panicked

and slid down the wooden ladder, filling my hands with splin-
ters as I went. I threw tripods and light stands out of the way
to get to David. I pulled him out of the mess. His face was
covered with shards of glass. There was a large gash in his
neck and blood was spurting out with every pump of his
heart. It looked like an artery had been severed.

"David! David!" I yelled crazily.

I tried to cover the gash with my hand. The cut was too
large and too deep. The pressure only made the blood squirt
between my fingers even faster. David gripped my arm and
gagged. He tried to speak, but couldn't. He convulsed for
thirty seconds or so before dying. His blank gaze stared up at
me accusingly as his grip relaxed.

I stood up. I was covered in David Rink's blood. Suddenly
I heard a noise from the front door of the loft. I looked over.
Morrie Fein, the fat sycophant with the funky glasses, was
standing in the doorway, a look of horror on his face.

"Holy shit," Morrie said with a shaky voice. He turned on
his heels and ran out of the loft. I staggered forward, grabbed
my pistol off the floor, and sprinted after him. I wanted to stop
him long enough to explain that what he saw was an accident.
Maybe I could work something out with him. A bribe, a deal,
something.

As I exited the loft I saw that Morrie was already far down
the street, standing beside a black BMW, fumbling with a key
ring loaded with keys, trying to find the proper one for the
car door.

"Hold it!" I yelled.

Morrie said, "Shit!" and slammed his hand against the driver's door window, trying to break the glass. He just managed
to set off the car alarm.

Morrie spun and ran down the deserted city street. I chased after him.

"Hold it, you fuck!" I screamed.

Morrie ran as hard and fast as he could, which, for an overweight guy, turned out to be pretty speedy. I barely managed to keep pace.

"I'll shoot you!" I yelled. "I swear to God I'll shoot you!"

Morrie overturned some trash cans in my path. I couldn't stop my momentum. I smashed into the cans and went airborne. I came down hard and skidded across the pavement, tearing the hell out of my right knee.

Morrie was running toward an alley. If he made it he would be safe. He would tell everyone what he saw. I looked up from the ground and realized that the eyewitness to what would appear to be a murder I had just committed was about to get away.

"Stop!" I screamed.

Morrie didn't miss a step. He didn't even pause. He was almost to safety. I aimed for Morrie's legs and opened fire with the Beretta. My aim sucked. Bullets ricocheted off the walls of the alley. Morrie got hit in the leg. He stumbled, and a second shot caught him in the center of his back. He let out a sharp yelp as he disappeared into the darkness of the alley.

I got to my feet and half staggered, half ran to the alley. I was terrified of what I would find. Morrie was on the ground, trying to crawl away, but there was not a lot of life left in him. He had a big red hole in his back. I turned him over and looked at his face. The man was about to die. His breathing was labored. Blood was trickling out of his mouth. When he spoke the words were gurgles.

"Oh shit, man," I said. "I'm sorry . . . I didn't mean it. . . ."

"You *shot* me!" Morrie cried. "How could you *not* mean it?"

"I just wanted to stop you from running."

"Good job."

I could hear sirens far in the distance. The area was sparsely populated, but the people who rented or owned lofts around here were primarily artistic night owls. Plenty were up at this hour. The 911 lines at LAPD must have been flashing like crazy.

"Hold on, man," I said. "Help's coming."

"I'll wait here," Morrie said. He laughed at his own joke and blood dribbled out of his mouth onto his shirt. The light in his eyes was starting to fade. He coughed and spit out a gob of bile and blood. I opened Morrie's collar so he could breathe easier.

"Gimme a cigarette," Morrie said.

I produced a cigarette and put it in Morrie's mouth.

"How about a light, asshole?" he asked.

In my confused state of mind I had neglected to light the thing. I fumbled with the lighter and fired up the cigarette. He took a deep puff and immediately started choking. I took the cigarette out of his mouth.

"What the hell are you doing here anyway?" I asked, trying to distract him from his fate.

"Mark sent me down . . . to check on Dave. . . . Been trying to call him all night. Mark knew you were on a rampage . . . 'fraid Dave might talk."

"You've gotta tell me what happened that night. How did they do it? How did they set me up?"

This made Morrie laugh again. And with the laughter came more blood.

"Set you up? You set yourself up."

"You rotten bastards. You were *all* in on it. Even Jennifer. I can't believe she'd fuck me over like this."

"Don't be so hard on JJ. She just thought Mark wanted to meet his idol. She didn't know what the real deal was."

"You used her to get to me?"

"That was the easy part. She didn't know shit about it. It's not her fault. You did it to yourself. . . . They knew your weakness. Pussy. They played you like a marked deck of cards. Mark wanted to get rid of Candice . . . wanted to get revenge on you. He asked her to do you . . . promised her some coke . . . told her to come to Nate's warehouse when she was done. She had no reason to suspect anything. Just another busy night in the life of a coke whore."

"You scumbags."

Morrie laughed even harder. This made him choke on his blood again. He started to shake violently. Panic filled his eyes. He was going into shock. I grabbed him, as if trying to hold the life in him. I didn't want it to happen again.

"Don't die! Don't die, you fuck! You've got to tell them the truth!"

The vibrations subsided and Morrie seemed to snap out of it. For a moment I thought he might even make it.

"What they said about you *was* the truth. . . ." Morrie gagged. "You *are* a murderer."

Morrie gripped my hand tightly. His back arched and stiffened. His eyes rolled back in his head and he projectile-vomited blood all over my clothes. He rolled over onto the ground and gradually relaxed like a tire with a slow leak. After a minute or so he was still. Steam exited his mouth in a steady stream. There were no pulsating breath patterns. He was dead. The heat was simply leaving his body.

I stared at Morrie Fein, transfixed by the process of death and the realization that I had brought about this process. He was right. I *was* a murderer.

didn't order me to get out of the car or put my hands on the steering wheel where he could see them. The fact that the car was a Lamborguini heading into Malibu probably didn't hurt matters. A guy in a Lamborghini couldn't have actually *killed* two people in the last hour, could he? I don't know why I was lying to the cop. It was only a matter of time before I would be arrested again. I just wanted a few more hours of freedom. I just wanted to go to my own home and lie down in my own bed for one last time.

"Please let me pass, officer," I continued. "I've got to get my dogs. Surely the fire won't go all the way to the beach."

"There's no telling with these winds. It's already blown across Mulholland Drive and Topanga Canyon pass. The flames are a hundred and fifty feet high in some places."

"I'll just get my dogs and come out. I can't leave them there. They'll go crazy."

"What kind of dogs do you have?"

"Huskies. Two of them."

"I love huskies. They're great animals."

"They're part of our family. My wife and my little girl will kill me if anything happens to them." I was beginning to enjoy the deception. I was creating a fantasy life right there in front of the big cop. A wholesome life that I felt good talking about, even if it was all bullshit. Jennifer Joyner's white picket fence was not in my future.

"Where is your family right now?" he asked, genuinely concerned.

"With friends in Santa Monica. They're probably worried sick about me."

The cop stared at me, trying to decide if he should give in.

"Tell you what," he said. "I'll let you through. Get your dogs and get out of there as quickly as you can. You never know.

Anyone stops you just tell 'em you're a freelance reporter and you've lost your ID. Those jerks have carte blanche around here."

"Thanks, officer. You've been most kind."

"Hey, I've got dogs too."

That's what I had been banking on. What cop didn't? He waved me through and shouted to the other cops up ahead to let me pass. Three fire engines and an ambulance ripped past me before I could get up to speed again.

As I pulled up to my row of houses along PCH I could see Robert Momberg in his driveway loading his Range Rover with supplies and precious keepsakes. Judgment Day had arrived after all. Robert had just the right vehicle to escape the fiery Armageddon working its way over the mountains.

I pulled my car into the garage and shut off the engine. Robert Momberg came running over, yelling my name, but the garage door descended in front of him before he could breach the entrance, cutting him off in midsentence. I didn't want to discuss evacuation plans with any soap-opera actors.

I sat staring at the garage wall, looking for an answer to my situation hidden in the grain patterns of the wood. Nothing was there. There were no answers to be had. I was thoroughly fucked and I knew it. I leaned my head back against the seat and stared at the ceiling. It had been the roughest of all nights in a series of *very* rough nights.

I entered the house and turned the kitchen light on. I was totally exhausted. Dried blood caked my clothes. I pulled the Beretta out of my jacket. It dangled at the end of my arm as I walked toward the living room. There were fresh groceries spread out all over the kitchen counter but I was too dazed to consider the implications. I shuffled like some zombie out

of a bad horror movie. I aimlessly entered the living room and
noticed that the lights were already on.

A voice suddenly shouted, "FREEZE!"

I looked up, shocked.

Lieutenant Archibald Di Bacco and two plainclothes detectives were standing in the living room. Di Bacco's cops had
guns drawn and aimed directly at my head. Detective Thompson was noticeably absent. I guess even cops sleep once in a
while.

Jennifer Joyner sat on the couch, eyes red from crying. She
stared at me in amazement, too shocked to speak. The video
tape of Candice Bishop's murder sat on a corner table beside
her. It was wrapped in a clear plastic bag marked EVI-
DENCE. I realized in an instant what had happened. Like
an idiot, I had left the tape in the machine and Jennifer had
come home with groceries for breakfast, lunch, or dinner
and had played the video while waiting for me. She put two
and two together, came up with five, and called the cops. I
might possibly have been able to explain it all if I hadn't been
covered in blood.

"Drop the gun!" Di Bacco yelled.

I let the gun drop to the floor. I was speechless. I moved
my arms in a futile, searching gesture, trying to say something,
but I couldn't get anything out. I must've looked like Franken-
stein's monster, desperately trying to communicate articu-
lately, but failing. Finally I spit out, "I . . . I can explain. . . ."

I looked at myself in a nearby mirrored wall. My clothes
were disheveled, torn, caked with blood, a pistol was at my
feet. A murder weapon. I could explain. Sure, buddy. The lu-
nacy of it all suddenly hit me. I let out a sickened snort of a
laugh. I was totally finished and I knew it.

I wondered for a moment where the people who had done

this to me were. What were they doing this very instant? Nate Boritzer was probably sitting alone in the middle of his stinking warehouse, getting ripped and staring up through his skylight at the moon. Of course I knew where David Rink and Morrie Fein were. David lay dead in our old loft. Morrie was in the alley a couple of doors down. The cops and paramedics were probably already zipping them up in little black body bags.

Mark Pecchia. What about Mark Pecchia? The sick mastermind behind the whole sordid affair. I could just picture him, banging teenyboppers and doing coke off their butts in celebration. I'm sure he was very satisfied. Very content. I had cleaned up a lot of loose ends for him. Candice. David. Morrie. All of them were security risks. They were gone now and I was to blame. Could Mark Pecchia have planned it all? Even the deaths of David Rink and Morrie Fein? Was he that smart? That Machiavellian? Had I been used not just as a scapegoat for Candice Bishop's murder, but also as a weapon to clear up some bad business? I would never know for sure, but I was certain that Pecchia could not have been happier with the outcome. I could just picture the reptilian smile he'd have on his face when he heard the news of what transpired this night.

And now I was smiling too, but it wasn't a satisfied smile. It was more of an idiot's grin. Or the look a man might have on his way over the edge.

The show was over.

This wasn't the first time a shitstorm had started over a dead bimbo and I was sure it wouldn't be the last time either. I just never thought I'd get caught the way I got caught. But then again, who ever does?

"Who'd you murder this time, Gardner?" Di Bacco asked. "Where do we look for the body?"

"I killed two of the guys who killed Candice Bishop. It was accidental. Both of them."

"I see," Di Bacco said skeptically. He was never going to believe this story. If I were in his place, I wouldn't either.

A knock came at my front door. One of the detectives went over and opened it. A uniformed policewoman stood in the doorway.

"Lieutenant Di Bacco," she said, "you better evacuate the area. The winds have shifted in this direction. The fire is only a mile away. We've got to get out of here."

"Soon," Di Bacco said.

The woman closed the door. Di Bacco turned and looked at me with that self-righteous glare of his.

"Anything you want to say before we take you in?" Di Bacco asked. "I know you got a right to an attorney and all, but I'd personally like to hear what you've got to say before your handlers get hold of you. Off the record, of course. It's professional curiosity. I've never seen one quite like you. Why'd you do it? You were on easy street. Why'd you screw it up? What makes a guy like you tick? Was life just so goddamned easy for you that you got bored?"

I stared at him for a long moment, trying to think of something to say. I had so much to tell him, so much to explain, but it was useless.

"You'd never believe me, Lieutenant," I said. I was starting to get calm now, accepting my fate.

"You're probably right," Di Bacco said. He nodded at the two detectives. "Cuff him and read him his rights, nice and fresh. We don't want any fumbles on this one."

By the time we left the house the fire had engulfed the mountain a hundred yards north of our block. Robert Momberg was long gone. Dozens of fire engines and emergency vehicles had pulled back and created a new front nearby. Reporters scurried among the firefighters, making their jobs that much easier. Hot ashes were coming down like red-and-white snowflakes.

A group of teenagers decked out in retro wear were dancing in the middle of the street amid the ashes and firehouse spray. A boom box near their feet was blasting away. I recognized the song as the Cult's "Sanctuary." You gotta love it when stuff like that happens.

"Better take Ms. Joyner out of here in her own car," Di Bacco said to one of the detectives. "This whole place looks like it's going to go up."

The detective started to pull Jennifer away from us, but she shrugged him off long enough to ask me one question.

"Why?" she pleaded.

I looked at her, wanting to convince her of the truth, wanting her to know that I didn't kill Candice Bishop, wanting to touch her if my hands weren't been cuffed behind my back. But what would be the point? Why drag her any further into this mess? I needed to free her. I looked at the cop as he took her by the arm again. He was a handsome, square-jawed guy in his thirties. He'd help her get over me.

"Have fun," I said. I smiled, trying to appear cavalier. I probably just looked crazy to her. That would be fine as well.

Jennifer stared at me with horror and burst into a new set of tears. The cop put his arm around her shoulders and led her to her little Fiat, which was parked across the street from the house.

Di Bacco glared at me for my lack of sensitivity.

"You're all heart, Gardner," he said.

"Don't I know it," I replied.

The cop put Jennifer in the passenger seat of her car and said a few comforting words. Then he scurried around to the driver's side and got in, nervously fumbling with her car keys. He was obviously excited by his new assignment. Definitely the right man for the job. Maybe Jennifer would get the white picket fence after all. And a shotgun to protect it with.

The house at the far end of our row had caught fire and was fully ablaze. Blown by the fierce Santa Ana winds, the flames were jumping the little six-foot gaps between the crowded buildings like Jesse Owens running the hundred in Berlin. The entire strip of houses would be on fire within minutes.

"Can I get my Lamborghini out of the garage?" I asked Di Bacco.

"Why?" he asked, as if it had been a ludicrous request.

I looked into Di Bacco's beady eyes and understood.

I wouldn't need a fast car where I was going.

"You're right!" I shouted over the growing noise of the flames and the firefighters, who were losing their valiant battle with nature. I looked at the expensive houses burning forty feet away from the trillions of gallons of water in the Pacific Ocean and started laughing uncontrollably.

"Gardner, you're a freak," Di Bacco said as he shoved me in the back of his plain-wrapped police car. They had parked under one of Robert Momberg's carports. That was probably what he was running over to tell me when I arrived. That'll teach me not to shut doors in my neighbors' faces. I'd try not to make the same rude mistake in prison.

An explosion rocked Teddy Vincent's house, raining flaming debris all over the area. God knows what he had in there. The firefighters scrambled and pulled back. One of them frantically yelled at us to evacuate the area. Good idea.

Burning embers were landing on the police car. Robert Momberg's house was going up quick. All those glossy eight-by-tens he had of himself must have made the perfect tinder. My house was starting to burn as well.

Di Bacco sat in the back with me and let the other cop drive. We pulled out and sped down PCH, away from Firestorm II. I looked back and watched the flames engulf my house. The firefighters were abandoning the area. They had given up. The row of beach houses was now just one long inferno. That strip of real estate alone would amount to roughly thirty million in damages to the insurance companies. They would probably manage to slip out of at least half their debt, one loophole or another. They certainly wouldn't pay *me* unless some judge forced it out of them. And that was growing unlikely. I didn't expect to be meeting many sympathetic judges in the near future.

I watched over my shoulder as the burning houses faded from view. I was going to jail, but actually I was heading for a kind of freedom. The last decade had been my own private prison. A prison of my own design. I hadn't really been alive. I had been acting tough and emotionally distant to protect myself and the people around me from my past. But I should have remembered one of the most dangerous risks inherent in photography.

If you pose long enough, you become the picture.